Read to Me

WITH
EARS TO HEAR
AND
EYES TO SEE

I0667740

THIRTY-TWO BRIEF STORIES
BY
UYLESS BLACK

READ TO ME
With Ears to Hear and Eyes to See
BY
UYLESS BLACK

Available at online booksellers and local bookstores

To communicate with the author:
Ublack7510@aol.com

For additional information on works by Uyless Black
Blog: Blog.Uylessblack.com
Web: www.UylessBlack.com
Facebook: Uyless Black Books
Pinterest: Uyless Black Books, https://www.pinterest.com/uylessblackbook

Information and Entertainment Institute
9323 N. Government Way, #301
Hayden, Idaho 83835

ISBN: 978-1-62737-012-7

Publicist: S. G. Mahoney
Cover & Book Design by Arrow Graphics, Inc.
info@arrow1.com
Printed in the United States of America

DEDICATION

*For my son, Tommy
and my brother, Tom*

CONTENTS

PREFACE

My son, Tommy, and I started reading to each other early in his life. While I read, he would follow my words as I pointed to the text with my finger. This guidance helped his learning new words, even though, many years ago, my first grade teacher had forbidden her students to finger read. Nonetheless, my son would do the same for me as he read. Thus, we read with both ears and eyes.

Each night, I would put him to bed earlier than my time for sleep. His only protest, and not much of a protest, was, "Read a story." That we did…together, often pausing to discuss a passage in the narrative.

For a while in the evening, we would lie together on the bed, propped up on pillows, as we educated each other, slowly and casually reading short stories and novels of adventure and heroes' exploits.

It is satisfying to learn how we can gain pleasure from reading as well as watching others' recite their cadence of passages. But this experience comes about if we do not read and listen too impatiently; that we study, if only a little bit, even casually, the structure of the author's compositions as seen by us—and as seen by those to whom we read.

Watching Tommy's reading those passages helped me gain an increasing appreciation of the written word, and I hope I did the same for him.

In grade school, after lunch, our teacher would have us rest our heads on our arms as she read us a story. I recall those times as ones of a mentally peaceful osmosis. When I awoke, I was refreshed and was certain I was wiser.

A few weeks ago, I was dining out with my wife, Holly. She uses a smart phone. I use a flip phone—a dumb phone. My phone is a blessing as I cannot do texting or Twitter while dining (or at any other time). Instead, I converse with my dining partner.

I conducted an informal visual survey at the eatery. About one-third of the customers, sitting with their friends and relatives, were involved in exercising their thumbs, all the while resting their tongues and ears, and ignoring their dinner companions.

It must be that the use of social media is addictive. In which case it baffles me why it is called "social." It degrades our interactive, face-to-face, voice-to-voice communications with one another. It requires only eyes to see, but not ears to hear. And the "seeing" is hurriedly constructed semi-sentences to remote viewers. Try sharing a Crème Brule and a sip of wine with a cell phone user.

I am not fond of the social media climate. Its emphasis on abbreviated communications, often hostile discourse to display egos, indifference to the beauty of language and our country's traditions and history are disturbing. The system is unraveling. It discourages the glue that binds Americans together to a common purpose: the bonding to one another with the associated ties of empathy and tolerance.

Near our winter home in Palm Springs, several of our neighbors have formed a book club. They often read passages from books to one another. I was asked to join the group to discuss some of my work and to read some passages from this work. They all share in the stories and have lively conversations about many topics. No television. No cell phones (as far as I could discern), as their attention was devoted to one another.

When I read my ancestors' letters, written during the American Civil War days, I am struck by their compositional beauty, by their tolerance toward others, even their enemy at that time. Today, even within our democracy, people who have genuine, but different views are excoriated in social media. They are demeaned as aliens to others' ideologies.

Forsaking reading and writing at the risk of over-using social media carries the risk of alienation. Let us attempt to communicate with a degree of empathy toward others, perhaps even reading to one another. I hope you will try this experiment with the stories in this book: Read them to someone. Have them read to you.

One never knows, it might actually lead to a conversation.

CHAPTER 1

THE PASTURE MORTICIAN

A rare rain storm across the pastures of the
southwest high plains startled plants and animals alike. The plants, accustomed to weeks,
sometimes months, without rain would soon
open their hidden undergrowth to show unexpected gifts,
expanding into a magnificent display of color and variety.
The animals would scurry for shelter but soon come forward
to drink the precious liquid.

The child especially liked roaming the pasture after such
a rain. The usually dry air transported moisture across the
thirsty grass and mesquite bushes. His awareness of its
humidity on his body brought forth a strange, pleasant sensation and for a short while, disavowed the dryness of the land.
He especially took pleasure in the smell of the pasture after
a rain. It was as if the water coming down to the earth had
evoked a clean yet pungent aroma from the thankful ground.

He ventured into this pasture often. It was named the
House Pasture, because the ranch house, barns, main corrals,

and windmill were located on this grazing land. The grazers of the prairie grass were cattle and sheep. The ranch hands rotated these animals to and from other pastures to accommodate their eating habits. Cattle ate parts of the grass. Sheep went after other parts.

The child paid little mind to the domesticated stock, other than tending to a few chores relating to their care. His main interest was the wildlife. He considered himself the pasture's game warden for toads, turtles, rabbits, foxes, lizards, ants, centipedes, coyotes, bugs, horned toads, prairie dogs, snakes, and other residents.

His sightings of foxes and coyotes were rare, but on occasion they came around, staying at a safe distance to check out this strange visitor. He was careful to avoid most snakes, but would pursue the shy bull snake. As it slithered away from him, he would hasten his walk to stay with its escape efforts. He was appreciative of this snake. It was an archenemy of the dangerous rattlesnake, another pasture citizen.

He often left the ranch house to walk this pasture to visit with the local wildlife citizens. Being much younger than his brothers, who were too grown-up to spend time with him, he selected his own playmates. The pasture patrons were not aware of this partnership, but it did not matter to the boy. He was glad for their company.

Turtles were one of his favorite companions. They maintained their quarters at a dirt pond placed in the House Pasture, a windmill-fed watering hole for the livestock. It was one of the few places in the pasture with trees. The boy often tracked down a couple turtles and carried them to the shade of his favorite tree. There, he would pick them up, marvel at their anatomy, and later put them down, hoping for a race as they made their way back to their aqueous sanctuary.

The title of game warden did not convey fully the scope of the child's activities in the pasture. And game warden might have meant this warden was the overseer of hunting. He did not hunt his game, other than to hunt for their whereabouts.

On occasion, his role of game warden had him come to the aid of his denizens. But those times were rare. The wild life tended to avoid humans and take care of themselves. Still, the boy had, on more than one occasion, tried to help an injured member of his domain.

He considered another of his responsibilities to be that of the pasture mortician. Be it a toad or turtle, when he came upon any dead body, he buried it.

The boy had adapted the burial ritual after attending his first funeral, that of his grandfather. He was especially impressed with the ceremony at the gravesite. He was surprised to learn the coffin accompanied his grandfather to the grave. He wanted to ask his father why a coffin could not be saved for other funerals. After all, his grandfather no longer had any need for it. But he suspected his question might provoke a curt answer, so he kept his opinion to himself.

For his own burial ceremonies on the pasture, more often than not, the body of the creature had been a meal for other critters, so he contented himself with burying partial bodies. He dug a shallow hole with a stone or stick, placed the remains into the grave, covered it up, and went about his business of finding live bodies to amuse himself.

During one of his turtle races under a shade tree, he was startled when something hit his shoulder. It came from above him. Upon looking around, he discovered the descending projectile had been a baby bird. It had fallen from its nest and was likely only alive by virtue of its fall being absorbed by the boy. He had come across dead baby birds before, some falling or being pushed from their nests. But he had not come across one that was still living. He had a rare opportunity to care for a wounded member of his preserve. It deserved special attention.

The bird was a newborn. It was naked of feathers, and its eyes were closed. No burials here, the boy placed the tiny body into his shirt pocket and climbed the tree to look for a nest. Positioned directly above his former place in the shade and the now departed turtles, it was not difficult to find. The nest had other small birds, also newborns. The boy knew at least one of the parents was nearby. He deposited the bird in the nest and hurriedly climbed down.

The next morning, he left early for the pasture. He was anxious to learn if his rescue operation had been successful. It was not, as in the nest lay the dead baby bird. But no others. The other birds were gone. He never found out what happened to this tiny victim's brothers and sisters.

For now, he gathered the body and placed it in his pocket. At this time, he thought about the coffin at his grandfather's funeral. He decided to change one aspect of his mortician's practice. He climbed down from the tree, walked back to the ranch house, and secured a match box from the kitchen. He then returned to the pasture, where he placed the bird in the match box. Finding a nearby stick, he dug a grave, placed the match box in the hole, and covered it up.

This burial, like that of his grandfather, was special. A coffin was in order.

CHAPTER 2

GAUGES

The gauge recorded the depth of the contents of the box. Filling-up the box as measured by the gauge had to be accurate. Fill the box to the top—no more, no less. If the gauge was set too high, reflecting an overflow from the box, there would be a waste of the box's contents. If set too low, with not enough contents, the gauge's box would not be filled, and the vacant space would be squandered.

After filling the box, the man would place a tick mark on the side of the box. An altered tick mark would then measure the contents of the box each time it was depleted. With this approach, he would reap the pleasure of an accurate measurement of the contents inside the box.

But life was complex. Life was more than one gauge. Living with one gauge meant living a single-dimensioned life. A full life required many boxes, many gauges.

Thus, for his life to be complete, he created numerous boxes and their associated contents. He began this task by measuring them full, reflecting the respective box's contents.

He believed the gauges would reflect his life's time on earth.

The man also came to believe his boxes and the accuracy of their gauges dictated—not only his time to live—but his daily activities. They reflected life's silent refrain. Each box would be aligned with what was transpiring in his day-to-day existence.

This mantra became his dictum. It became an idea providing guidance on how to live his life. It gave him peace.

From that initial time, after his boxes had been topped-off, he began to remove their fillings, pulling them out and using them. As a consequence of his needs, he lowered the tick marks of the gauges on the boxes, reflecting their shallower contents.

While setting up his boxes and gauges, he made a calculation. Once filled, the boxes would keep him going until he died. As he used their contents, the ticks on the sides of the boxes marked the time he had to live and when he was to die. As the contents diminished, he placed the tick marks toward the bottom of each side of the box, recording and reflecting their depleting nature.

He knew the boxes would not empty at the same time, so the first tick mark that took place at the bottom of one of the gauges would signal his release from using the other gauges and boxes to measure his time to live. It was a logical approach: Use many gauges, but depend on the first mark that reflected an empty box, the one that would determine his ending his time on earth.

The man using these boxes was into his eighties. One might question why at this late time in his life, he had chosen to create the gauges that measured the contents of his boxes and his remaining time to live. His project was not a recent undertaking. He had filled the boxes and conceived of their gauges many years ago.

The discovery of his inventory came about because the man had died. His death was the result of a vehicle collision. His demise prompted the police to pay a call on the address listed on his driver's license, the location of his boxes.

It appeared he had lost control of his minibus. It slammed into a tree. The accident puzzled the police. Not the accident itself, which was rather common. The vehicle was an early 1970's vintage. It likely malfunctioned. What puzzled the police was their discovery of two replicas of the minibus in his garage. Same years, same models, same colors, but they were rusted, worn-out, no longer running.

Receiving no response to their door knocks, the police entered his house where they came across the two broken down vehicles in the garage. Inside the house, they found a place of happenstance trimming, one of less decoration than more.

They discovered each room in the house contained many boxes, each one with only one kind of content. One box was partially full of shoes, all of the same trade name and year. Another box contained sets of trousers of the same make. Another box had shirts of the same brand and model.

On and on, scores of boxes of different sizes in which the contents inside each box were identical to one another. One had a single type of shampoo; one housed a specific razor brand; one contained boxes of the same cereal; another, the same kind of canned fruit juice. One box contained an identical product for pain killers.

Each box had a vertical line drawn on one side, from the top of the box to its bottom. The boxes had varying numbers of horizontal tick marks drawn through the vertical lines.

One box was empty. The police never discovered if it had contained anything or why it alone was bare. They noted the vertical line on the side of the box had horizontal tick marks drawn from the top of the line to the bottom. The bottom mark was near the floor where the box rested.

Take only what you need. No less. No more. Stay structured. Stay within. Remain focused. Do not succumb. Keep it simple. After all, the war was complex enough.

CHAPTER 3

A BRIDGE

Some members of the family suspected, but none spoke of it. After years of silence, his younger brother had come to know for certain. After all, while visiting his older brother's four bedroom home several years ago, he discovered his brother shared a bedroom with a male friend. Counting the bedroom the younger brother slept in, that left two bedrooms vacant. The younger brother knew that ordinary men did not sleep with other men if additional accommodations were available. It was a simple deduction, even to a naïve teenager.

This discovery came about because the younger brother had made a surprise visit to his older sibling. He arrived late. His brother did not have time to scurry back into the closet. Still, nothing was said. The façade stayed intact.

It was past time to get it out in the open. For too long it had been hidden. The gap between his brother and his family had widened. The older brother was in his early thirties. Even at this age, he dared not bring his world into the world of his mother, brothers, sisters, and especially his father. If the older brother made such a bold gesture, he believed he would no longer be welcome in his home. He could not bear such ostracism. His family formed his soul, his defense against an outside world.

Nonetheless, society was gradually adjusting to accommodating a world such as his. And while his family embraced him as their son or brother, they had not adjusted to his way of life, at least in any demonstration of support. But they were not certain about this oldest sibling. They were imprisoned in a world of silent ignorance.

When the older brother was a youth, a male homosexual was not called gay. He was tagged as queer. In the family's small hometown of those days, gays pretended to be something or someone else. This act was not only for maintaining their pride and avoiding society's so called shame, it was also to safeguard their health. Had the older brother been found out, he and his family would have been silently ostracized. The boy might have been attacked by other males. Others had been beaten-up because they were different. Why would this boy be an exception?

While in his late teens, to avoid pain to his loved ones and to himself, the older brother moved away. His confining world had paid him a silent call, with the tacit advice to remove himself from the straits of the society surrounding him and his family. He eventually found a more understanding culture in a faraway place. There, he could live an honest and safe life.

The older boy's leaving home was met with contrived silence. With the exception of an increased quietness pervading the evening meal, the family's ostensible milieu remained largely unchanged. For fear of the father's reaction, the mother never broached the subject of the son's sudden departure. Of course, neither did the brothers and sisters openly speak of the self-exiled, self-proclaimed orphan. They knew only enough about the reason for their brother's departure to confuse them.

The youngest in the family, six years old at the time of his brother's exodus to friendlier soil, was oblivious to it all. He missed his brother, but his role was to be seen, not heard. He knew of no subject he thought of sufficient interest to others to bring up at the dinner table. But even at his young age, he was not oblivious to the sudden absence of anyone talking about the oldest child, a brother who was a hero to him and the other siblings.

Thus, few words were exchanged in this family about the young man's absence. After all, if the subject was never brought up, the daily goings-on, the routine chores of just getting past the evening meal, would keep the subject at a safe distance. Once broached, it would be out of the closet. No more whispers among the neighbors. Silent innuendo would be replaced by vocal rumor.

Things went this way for fifteen years. By this time, the former six-year-old child had reached manhood. Through these years, he witnessed his brother's growing isolation from an otherwise loving family. The father was a rough hewn cowboy, an image reflective of a taciturn, masculine Hollywood stereotype. He would have read *Brokeback Mountain* in surprised disbelief. He was not a mean man, just a person conditioned to believe that surely, his first son could not be one of those.

But his views did not mirror the attitudes of his wife or his children. They wanted the oldest son back. They were not sure about these matters of alternate sexual preferences. They were not even certain about their loved one's sexuality, a subject no one dared to discuss. Nonetheless, their uncertainty was secondary to their longing for the presence of his company.

As the boy grew older, the views of the dad had become irrelevant to his youngest child. Such is a son's rebellion against a father. Perhaps it was also attributable to the possibility that maturation is sometimes accompanied with empathy and understanding.

But there was more. The boy, now a man, had discovered the female body and mind. He came to revere both. As time went on, he continued to wonder why his brother was so different from him.

One day, he was ruminating about his brother's sexual ways of thinking. Through fate or fortune, he transported his mental wonderment for the female to the mind of a gay man: If the gay person had the same passion and awe for a male as he had for a female, how could anyone deny this human his desire and love? It would be akin to a straight male denying himself a female.

Thus, after his successful climb past puberty into manhood, the youngest of the lot made the decision to breech his family's isolation from his older brother. He decided to bring his brother out of the closet, to form a bridge from his brother to the brother's family.

He would start gradually, building the bridge piecemeal. To get a foot out of the closet, to make that first step, he would inform his older brother that he knew; that he did not care and in turn, he cared; that he was happy for his older brother; that he liked and respected his brother's chosen mate.

If all went well, he would ask his brother if the youngest in the family could act as the messenger to their parents and siblings, to be an emissary. The younger brother knew the older brother could not possibly face their father with this news. It was not in the cards. But the younger one could. After all, he would be the conveyor of the news, but he would not be the news itself.

It sounded simple in theory. But many theories crumble in the face of reality. He was nervous and hesitant. Habits die hard. Fears die harder. He was about to enter into his brother's private world, and ask his brother to reveal his world to public scrutiny; perhaps scrutiny that would lead to scorn. But he was determined on this visit to open the door. It was well-past time.

After the younger brother made known his open secret, the older brother turned to tears. Tears held in check for over thirty years. They were not tears of fear or shame. They were tears of joy. A bridge was under construction.

CHAPTER 4

GATE 4

*M*ost passengers sat patiently at gate 4. The more anxious were standing near the gate. All awaited to board a late arriving flight. They looked forward to the incoming plane disembarking its passengers, so the new passengers could be boarded and conveyed to the next inevitable intermediate stop.

The airport authorities had installed television sets at the gates. Each set played back the same news program. In turn, each program repeated itself. Sitting at any gate, one would gain a sense of the continuous replay of a so called news flash. After a while, the repetition became reminiscent of the *Groundhog Day* movie.

The current screen was displaying an interview. A journalist was asking a financial analyst about the increasing disparity of wealth between the "haves" and "have-nots" of society.

During this exchange, a cleaning cart arrived in the gate 4 area. It was pushed by an African American woman. Her hair was set in a short ponytail. Little more than a nub of hair, it assumed a parallel plane to the floor and a perpendicular attachment to her head.

The undersized ponytail spoke about its resolute wearer. She believed she was different from the other cleaning cart women who usually displayed a happenstance, disheveled hair style. To this cleaner, her curtailed, controlled hairdo offered a cosmetic reprieve from her lowly status as a collector of garbage.

She parked her cart near gate 4, in a location deferential to ongoing passenger traffic. There, she took out a broom and a dust bin from her cart. She began collecting flyers' discards; their former desiderata, however temporary. Part of a sandwich; magazines; crushed potato chips; used tissue. All came under the purview of her tools.

However modest, she took pride in her domain at the airline gates, as well as her modestly defiant hair-do. She picked up plastic cups, some empty, some full, some partially so. The same with drink bottles. The same with Styrofoam containers of partially discarded food. The same with practically everything she dumped into her cleaning cart. Little saved, much wasted.

Unlike some cleaners, she took care to separate the glasses and cups. After making sure each one was empty, she stacked them into their categories: one stack for plastic, one stack for styrofoam, another stack for cardboard. She was not required to be so caring with her payload, but it was her nature to tend properly to her consignment, her property.

She contemplated the fact that she could easily feed herself and her family on the cornucopia of waste that was at her disposal. Her wage-pay was $10.00 an hour. Her eight-hour day yielded $80.00. After assorted deductions, the net amount she took home was $60.00.

Across from gate 4 was a McDonald's outlet. After sale taxes were factored in, the price for a Big Mac meal was around $7.00 (or more). She was sufficiently versed in arithmetic to know that purchasing two Big Mac meals to satisfy her children's dreams was beyond her means. Her children's fanciful Big Mac burger, with French fries and a Coke on the side, would cost her some $14.00.

Fourteen dollars would eat into her daily earnings of sixty dollars. After all, there was rent to pay for her subsidized housing; money for public transportation back and forth to the airport and her home; clothes. Compensation for her mother was another drain on her meager income. The grandmother took care of the grandchildren while the mother worked. There was no man around. He was long gone.

Meanwhile, the television pundits at Gate 4 opined about the differences between the income of a Wall Street analyst and a minimum wage worker. As she swept crushed Fritos into the dust pan, the woman took in their comments. Still tending to her tasks of collecting trash, she listened and watched the interview. The pundits explained there was an income ratio difference of 100 to 1 in favor of the Wall Street worker over people such as trash collection workers. In many cases, the disparity was much more. She was not versed in arcane ratios, but she knew a 100 to 1 figure was decidedly not in her favor.

Nor was she versed in high level finance. But she wondered, *100 to 1? What did they do to deserve that money?* As she picked up a Snickers candy wrapper, she glanced again at the television screen. The announcer informed his viewers a recent CEO of a Fortune 500 company had been fired for his inability to "turn the company around." His severance pay was twenty million dollars, as well as stock in the company that had recently disowned him. During his time at the bank, he made thirty million dollars a year. During the same time, the bank lost four billion dollars.[1]

She did not understand the machinations and nuances that lay behind the announcement made by the news commentator. But she did know she would have settled for a small fraction of the money this person had received in spite of his failures. She was not so clueless to know she did not have the skills equal to this former CEO. Still, she could not quite put her head around rewarding failure. But she was well aware if she lost her job, her compensation package would be a quick escort out of the airport and nothing more.

As she was cleaning gate 4, she wondered about the point of wasting the food she was throwing way. After all, it was tasty and safe. MacDonald's was certifiably clean. But she knew she risked losing her job if she were discovered hoarding the remnants of a sandwich from an airport fast food café.

During her putting finishing touches on gate 4, the financial expert on the television program was warming up. He warned that the growing discrepancy of peoples' wealth and income would lead to the disenfranchised rebelling against, as he framed it, the moneyed class.

During the time the woman was cleaning gate 4, the financial authority was cleaning his pipes and conscience. Upon completing the task, she decommissioned her broom. Putting it and the dust bin onto her cleaning cart, she released the cart's brake and proceeded toward gate 5.

As the television's sounds at gate 4 receded, the financial expert's exhortations still fell on the cleaner's distant ears. She was not a rebellious person nor bent on creating trouble,

---

[1]   The specific example of this CEO is Angelo Mozilo of Countrywide Bank. See Uyless Black, *The Nearly Perfect Storm*, IEI Press, 2012, 157. Available at Amazon.com.

but she cast a glance back to the screen at gate 4. The TV commentators were discussing how a person had made over one billion dollars in the stock market by betting against the stock market itself.[2]

The narrator used the word, "shorted" to describe how this man had made an incomprehensible amount of money.

She understood little about the pronouncements coming from the financial experts. Her job was to brush aside the discards, the junk of others' lives, into her dustpan. She made almost nothing for her efforts. She had no way of knowing that those identified on the television program made millions by doing the same: disclaiming the desiderata of others' lives. She did it with her cleaning cart. As the TV pundit said, they did it by going short. "Going short" was lost on her. Betting against something was beyond her mental composition.

The reader might ask: Who was more productive to society? The people, featured on the TV, who cleaned-out other peoples' wealth or this cleaning woman, who cleaned-out other peoples' trash? In other TV programs, it was argued both ways, but for the cleaning woman, she was unaware of these theoretical debates.

Her current disenfranchisement was soon to be remedied, if only partially. She had deposited in her cart a barely eaten Big Mac and several slices of pizza. Her ponytail was still erect. So was her spirit. The technical babble from the television commentators was not entirely lost on this woman. After all, she knew about the disparities of life all too well.

She decided she would take what was needed from her scavenging. And take it as the opportunity offered. Who knew what food might or might not be available at the next gate?

---

[2] Ibid., 244-245.

After all, she was bombarded with television proclamations: *Get it while you can.* Why couldn't she?

As she walked away from gate 4, the television set was highlighting another financial whiz. He was lamenting the rising resentment in America's land of plenty against those who were on welfare and freeloading on America's affluent population. The commentator railed against the deadbeats, those in the country who he said, "Sucked on the tits of those who created America's milk."

Being relatively uneducated, she did not fathom all the incantations of the TV moderators, but she did understand how much pleasure her children would have from a partially eaten Big Mac and slices of pizza. She reached into her bin, pulled out the food, and placed it into her pocket. It had been given up, so why should she not take over ownership for what was her consignment, her property.

After all, how was security to know she had shorted the garbage bin?

CHAPTER 5

A CLOSE SHAVE

"*T*hat's a lot of blood on that dress. Is your mother okay?"

"She's okay."

"What happened? A car accident? Haven't read about anything in the paper."

"She slipped on the porch steps...had a fall."

"Been to your home before. Don't recall that many steps on your porch."

"She slipped on the back porch."

"Fine, we'll give the dress cleaning a go, but tell your mom we may not be able to get all the stains out."

"Okay."

He raced to the door of the dry cleaners. He wanted to get as far away as possible from that dress, from its haunting presence, from its memories. He wanted to get as far away as possible from anyone who knew his mom did not suffer from a fall; away from anyone who might know or suspect he was lying to avoid embarrassment and humiliation.

His mother had instructed him to take her dress to the cleaners, "If they ask about the blood stains, tell them I had a fall from the porch steps." That was the story line.

Why was he the designated courier? It was not as if he had anything to do with the dress or the dried blood on it.

Yet he was shamed. Such is the guilt of the innocent: distress because of inexplicable self-reproach. The dry cleaners' owners knew him, his mother, and his deceased father. By carrying the dress to the cleaners, it was as if he had become the guilty party. But who else could do it? He was an only child. He would never have accepted his mother humiliating herself by taking a blood stained dress she owned to the cleaners. The beating she received that had bloodied the dress was degrading enough.

If anyone should have shown his face to the man at the cleaners, it was the man who assaulted his mother. His name was Frank, at least as far as anyone knew. He was one of several murky suitors who came around to call on his mother, sometimes announcing themselves before a visit but usually not.

They often arrived drunk. If they showed up sober, it was because they had not yet paid calls to the local bars. They had recently finished their shift in the oil fields and had driven into town, reeking from the grime they had picked up at the drilling rigs and crude-oil tanks.

The child's hometown was a rough place. Several years before, its once placid rural setting had been subsumed by the discovery of oil. The quiet community had been replaced by a raucous town. With oil, came oil men, some well intended, some unable to hold their liquor. Others were of a violent bearing, ready to be set off by the slightest provocation.

The beating of the boy's mother came easily to Frank. He had scared-off the other men, principally because he did not need whiskey to stoke his violence. It came naturally to him.

The man had the boy's mother to himself. No one else was around to protect her except her ten-year old son.

While reading in his bedroom, the child was roused by his mother's screams. Entering the living room, he found no one. He followed the noise to the front yard. There he saw Frank standing over his blood-soaked, semi-conscious mother. "She asked for it kid. Get her into the house! Keep this to yourself or you'll get the same."

Dismissing the incident with a haughty wave of his hand, the man got into his car and drove away.

For a few moments, time froze. His mother lay on the bare ground in the open yard for what seemed an eternity. How could he help his mother? Who of his friends or relatives could help him? Yet how could he even think of calling for help? How could he allow anyone to see his mother in this condition?

Although not close to the size of his mother, he went about the task of righting the semi-conscious woman, getting her to her feet, where the two of them jointly staggered into the house.

Humiliation and fear overwhelmed him. He hoped a relative might drop in to visit and take care of the situation. He also hoped a town citizen had not been driving by to bear witness to the degradation of his family's name. All the while, he was scared that his mother was in harm.

Ordeals pass. Their events recede. His mother came to and somewhat to her senses. She raised herself from the living room floor, slowly walked into her bedroom, and closed the door. The child did not see her until the next day, the day he was assigned the job of taking the bloodied dress to the cleaners.

Later, on that same day, Frank came around, milling about as if nothing had happened.

The child knew his father would have put an end to the presence of this vile creature. It would have been short work. But then, if his father were alive, Frank would never have been a presence in the boy's life.

To see his father again! To have his father help his mother and him out of jams. To listen to his dad's stories, of his gentle gibes with his only child. To lather his father's face with shaving soap and take joy in their routine joyful banter, while he used a straight razor to shave his dad's face.

As he placed a warm towel over his father's eyes, he was reassured, "Someday son, you'll have a beard of your own. For now, you can practice on mine. Not too close, as usual. I like some growth, and say, did you hear the story about?..." As his hero's tales placed the boy into a world of imagination and fantasy.

This world no longer existed. His father had left farming and taken on a job in the oil industry. That's where the money was. While he and his crew were pulling pipe from a drilling hole, his father was knocked from the top of the rig. No more shavings, warm towels, or tall tales. His dad's razor lay in the medicine cabinet, the boy still too young to use it on this own face.

But the razor and its shaver were not idle. Frank was fond of the straight razor. The child was enlisted as the local barber to satisfy the resident sadist's preferences for a close shave. After delivering the dress to the cleaners and after Frank had returned to the scene of the assault, the boy was told to prepare soap, hot water, and a hot towel for Frank's shave.

"Same as before, Frank?"

"The usual, a close shave. You know that. Why ask now?"

Placing a warm, wet towel over Frank's eyes, the boy responded, "I just want to be sure this time."

CHAPTER 6

A SACK FULL OF KITTENS

*T*he feral cats on the ranch were a blessing and a blight. They kept the rodent population down, but the aggressive animals also attacked and killed chickens, especially baby chicks. They were effective and ferocious killers.

To compound the problem, feral cat colonies multiplied, as they had few predators to control their proliferation. On some ranches, the animals became bold enough to meander around the ranch house, hunting for game. They stayed out of reach of humans but were known to pounce upon unwary domestic cats, if only to hone their skills.

On occasion, a ranch's domestic cat would migrate into the feral cat population. While this was rare, it was of concern to the cat's owners, who considered their pets as part of the human family.

The domestic cats also presented problems, but of a different kind. Unless preventative measures were taken, the cats multiplied profusely. Neutering (spaying) was usually not undertaken, as it required taking the animal to a vet, who resided many miles away.

One of the humans on such a ranch was a child who adored cats. He learned the resident adults on the ranch practiced a draconian form of feline birth control: killing newly born cats. He was unaware of this form of extermination until one of his favorite pets gave birth to a litter of six kittens.

The boy spent much of his time observing and playing with these kittens. The mother had no objection. She and the boy had formed a bond long before the births of her babies took place.

The mother had chosen an inappropriate place to nurse her newly born kittens: in a small building called the washhouse. There, a Maytag washer, tubs, and wringers were set up to clean the clothes of the ranch's family and hired hands.

The washhouse was too busy for this feline family. Indeed, the kittens were in danger of being stepped on or even kicked around. To some of the ranch hands, cats were a nuisance. But they were not a nuisance to the child. In a mutual act of trust and kindness, the mother cat allowed the boy to relocate her kittens and her to the sheep barn. At this time of the year, this building was vacant.

The mom had made her home on top of some clothes destined for the Maytag. Ever so gently, the lad scooped down underneath their bed, picked the animals up, and carried them a few hundred feet to their new home. There, they would be safe, or so he thought.

A few weeks after the kittens were born and had been transported with their mother to their new home, they were close to ending their time on the tit. Soon, their mother would wean them away from her milk. It was at this time that their sanctuary was exposed.

A hired hand happened to come into the barn and

discovered the boy, the mother cat, and the kittens. The man talked a while with the child and then went on his way to do his chores. Later, he mentioned to the boy's father about the encounter with his boss's son. The father did nothing at that time. The sentence for the cats came later that evening at the dinner table.

The father was not angry, but resolute. He explained to his son that another litter of cats would end-up creating even more litters of cats. He explained one pair of cats, their litters, and their litters' litters would eventually result in hundreds of cats running around the ranch house area in just a few years. The family could not take care of an ever increasing cat population, many of which would join the feral community and would continue to decimate the chickens.

The child marveled at the wisdom of his father, even though he did not fully grasp the mathematical implication of cats having kittens and their proliferation of litters.

The boy was ordered to get rid of the kittens the next day. The momma cat could remain, as she was a treasured member of the family. The father proclaimed the cat should not have let herself get pregnant in the first place, as if she had control over her natural behavior.

Get rid of the kittens? The boy had no idea what his father meant. At this point he was instructed what to do by one of the hired hands who was at the dinner table. He remonstrated, in so far as a child can protest to a formidable father. But to no avail.

That night was one of near sleepless anguish, even for a sleep-filled child. What could he do? His father had issued a decree and such orders were not to be disobeyed. Finally, near dawn, he fell into an unwelcome slumber.

Come the morning, the child went to the sheep barn. In his hands were a sack, a rock, and some string. He also carried a small container of milk. He had been sneaking milk to the mother cat each day for several weeks.

The feline family unit was glad to see him. As before, he brought sustenance and companionship, essentials for the well-being of any animal.

He watched the mother lap up the milk. He watched her children take it into their mouths, secondarily through their mother's tits. After a while, he gently picked up each kitten and placed it into the sack, where he had placed the rock.

That done, he tied the sack at the top with the string. He lifted the sack, while the mother looked up at him with seeming curiosity but without alarm. After all, he was a trusted member of her entourage.

Filled with confused meowing kittens and one large rock, the child carried the sack to a nearby pond. He stood there for a long while.

Finally, he sat the sack down. He untied the string and let the kittens out onto the ground. They remained confused, but stopped their vocal protests. They began to explore their new surroundings, wandering away in different directions.

The boy knew their chances of survival were small, but certainly better than a sure-fire watery grave. He knew he could not return them to their mother, which would lead to their certain death and the wrath of his father. His action was his only choice. He rationalized they were still kittens, but not floundering babies.

Who knows? Younger creatures had survived in the wild. They may find their way into the feral community. A motherless female adult cat might take them on. Those were the boy's hopes.

The child kept the kittens' escape a secret. He would never reveal to the adults on the ranch that the sack he tossed into the pond contained only a rock.

CHAPTER 7

THE EXISTENTIAL LIFE
OF COWBOYS

A herd of 3,000 longhorns has bedded down. The animals are restive and miserable. During the day, they have been winding across a barren prairie toward a railhead up north. For now, they are huddled together, in collective defense, to keep themselves from icing-over.

The cold and wet weather came up without warning. The trailing to the railhead is taking place during early winter, and climate conditions do not take into account the schedules of cattle drives.

The herd will endure another ice cold night on the Great Plains. Come the morning, they will look for a hint of heat from a rising sun, a spot of food from the sparse prairie grass, a lick of water from a nearby nearly frozen river.

The cattle remain impervious to their adversities. They survive on sparse grass and little water, as they have no choice. The drovers are driving them to a place they would not have chosen. Thus, they have meandered up a northern route in western America, one dictated by the cowboys.

These drovers, the cowboys who are herding the cattle north, are not in much better shape. They are also miserable. Sleeping on the frozen ground, looking for the same allusion of relief as the cattle, they are little more than a horse blanket away from freezing to death.

Two cowboys are assigned to look over the cattle each night, to keep them in a manageable assemblage. This night duty, while chillingly miserable, is not difficult. The cattle are in need of rest and have settled in for the night.

The cowboys often rouse a sleeping steer. As the disgruntled animal is prodded from its repose to slowly stand and walk away to find another nearly freezing place to rest, one of the cowboys dismounts his horse and lies down in the warm bed made by the large animal. Covering himself with a blanket, he finds relief in a brief moment of comfort.

His drover partner, the other night-riding cowboy, stands watch over his friend and the herd, knowing he will be next in line to rob a steer of its temporary escape from the cold. He will then feel the warmth left by the displaced steer, a fleeting comfort coming from outside the cowboy's own body.

On winter's Great Plains, warmth is a luxury, offering short lived succor. Nonetheless, the steer's former bed offers a brief respite from the dreaded assignment of drawing the night duty of overlooking a valuable herd of cattle. Dollars are in store for these lowly drovers, and many more dollars are in store for the cattle owners.

The title holders of these cattle are not part of this trek. Presently, they lie sleeping in New York City suites; just as likely in Paris hotels—comfortably reposed between silk sheets covered with warm wool blankets. With cow skin rugs on the floor, they proclaim their love of the rugged life on the Great Plains.

As they enter near-slumber, the smell of these hides gives them peace with their view of the natural order of life. They've won yet another battle for existential survival in a cold world—with ample heat in their rooms, thanks to radiators.

The cowboys hunkering in on the frozen southwest plains struggle to survive their unforgiving landscape. A few moments of respite underneath horse blankets from the unrelenting cold gives them a dollop of hope. Come the morning, like the cattle they herd, they will look for a hint of heat from the rising sun, a spot of food from their sparse knapsack, a sip of water from the grudging river.

The cowboys are no different from other humans who wish to live in comfort, but they must remain stoic to their hardships. As with the longhorns, they have no choice. They need money, so they are also headed for a place not of their choosing.

At the railhead, where the cattle will be forced into train cars destined for the slaughter house, the drovers will be given their wages for the drive. Not a lot, but enough to pay off gambling debts, buy some whiskey and women. Then, come better weather, they will head back south to join the next cattle drive north.

Meanwhile, the two cowboys stay alert to keep the cattle intact and calm. Their trail mates are resting at their nearby campsite, taking in food, coffee, and conversation. As the last embers of the cowboys' campfire take flight into the cold western air, the drovers prepare themselves for another night of gloom. As they finish their beans and biscuits, they exchange a few observations about their situation on this trail, as well as their lives.

One cowboy, we call him Jim, begins, "You know, boys, I've been thinking about this trail we're on. Seems to me we are riding our horses and driving these longhorns into a hostile universe."

The cowboys nod their heads in agreement. They have discovered that life on the trail is devoid of meaning. It is purposeless, empty, and for this cattle drive, cold as hell.

Another cowboy joins in, "Well, these plains are empty, that's for sure. And I share your insight, Jim. This wretched place where we've been herding these cattle is indifferent to human existence. And our getting shot at by Indians is just plain inexplicable. Those arrows and bullets going around me and my horse yesterday was a surreal experience, out of this world."

Jim's cousin, Tom, also joins in, "Jim, our grandma warned us about this drover business. She told us about freedom of choice and all. She said cattle-driving was up to us, that we humans, even cowboys, have the freedom of making decisions about our existence."

Jim replies, "Tom, are you talking about taking responsibility for what we do? Is that your point? Are you being fancy again?"

Tom, "Being fancy? If I am 'to be' anything, I must first experience 'being' and search for the meaning of life. Only then can I come 'to be.' Jim, your problem is you don't know a hill of beans about the difference between 'to be' and 'being.'"

Jim shivers from the cold and from Tom's chilly reception to his ideas. He responds, "I sure as hell do know the difference. 'To be' is what I am going to be at the end of this cattle drive. And 'being' is what I am doing to get there. It's pretty simple: I am 'to be' in order 'to be being.' And I'll tell you something else. I know that existence precedes essence. Right now, my existence is miserable out here, and that's the essence of my life."

Having finished his meager plate of food, Tom is laying out his equally meager bed, "Hell fire, Jim, You got your philosophy plumb backwards. Plato said that essence *precedes* existence."

At this time, a sudden thunderstorm comes into the area, interrupting the cowboys' ruminations on life. The flashes of lightning, accompanied with sudden winds and a near freezing torrential rain, panics the longhorns. The huge herd of cattle stampedes, running over Jim, Tom, and the other cowboys' now-doused campfire. Trying to stave off freezing to death, the nighttime drovers who were overlooking the herd made the mistake of hunkering down together in a steer's former bed. Crushed by hundreds of hoofs, they become indistinguishable from the frozen landscape.

Existence is gone. So is its essence. So is Jim. So is Tom. So are the other cowboys.

Far away, an existential maverick is alive and well. Similar to the cowboys in this story, he is a being of individuality. He lives in Paris. Unlike the drovers, his safe essence lives on. Secure in the cocoon of a metaphysical subsistence, he debates his place on earth and in the cosmos. His warmth need not be self-generated. It is amply furnished by the furnaces in his apartment and that of his heated readers. They are stoked by his fiery mental meanderings. In its essence, his metaphysical comfort exists.

Suddenly, this Sartre-like person is removed from an intellectually pointless illusion to a physically hostile reality. He is transported—existentially speaking, of course—from his mentally disputed subsistence to a bodily challenged existence; from a coddled and safe Paris to a frozen, dangerous cattle trail on America's Great Plains.

In the middle of the night, he stands alone on a frozen barren plateau, realizing he is surrounded by a herd of stampeding, deadly cattle and an even deadlier nature. His existence swiftly becomes one of essence—existentially speaking, of course.

CHAPTER 8

BEACH ASSAULT

The son had witnessed what can happen to a man during an amphibious assault against a well-armed enemy. His father's platoon was in one of the first amphibious boats to land at Utah Beach on D-Day. The WWII veteran suffered no physical wounds. His were mental. In those days it was called battle fatigue. Later, it became known as post traumatic stress (or post traumatic stress disorder). His dad left for Europe as a fully functioning man. He returned to America as a stranger to himself and his family.

The father and his battle mates were pinned down on the beach for the better part of a day. Some of them were shot while wading through the surf trying to find cover. Some were wounded. Some drowned, weighed down by heavy gear. Once on the beach, his father watched his comrades take a bullet or more. One-by-one, they were killed or wounded. By the time his platoon could get off the beach, the son's father was barely capable of holding a rifle, much less fire it.

But his dad somehow managed to perform. Perhaps the routine of his training emasculated his fear. Perhaps his pride would not allow fear to strip him of his manhood. He stayed with it, but with each day of battle, his "fatigue" became more pronounced. He was awarded medals for his gallantry. By the time the awards were draped around his neck, he had retreated into a nether world of silent, crazed delusions.

The father never let others know he was, as they said in those days, a basket case. To suffer from battle fatigue was a sign of weakness. Many warriors, and brave ones at that, carried this malady for decades with grace and dignity. His father fit this bill to a T.

Some men are impervious to fear. Perhaps their mental armor is indifference, perhaps stupidity, as often as not, a rugged mentality toward life. Somehow, they are able to carry on with their duties and suffer no ill effects.

Others lose their power to act, to think rationally. Their once prideful independence is stolen by fear. They are not cowards. Perhaps they are victims of the genetic roll of the dice.

But given the history of his father, why would the son risk this dice roll?

Nonetheless, he volunteered for the Marines. The son signed up because he had to know. He could not go through life thinking he might not be as brave as his father; that unlike his hero dad, he might not perform courageously when he was half scared to death.

Hero? The son had grown weary of being called a hero for his exploits on the football field. Courageous? He was described as courageous for standing firm at the free throw line and sinking two shots to bring his team a championship. These ideas described his father, not the father's son. Or did they? He had to find out.

The operation was the first amphibious landing of Marines in the Vietnam War. It was a small assault, consisting of 1,500 Marines and supporting elements. Intelligence operatives informed the combat units that they might encounter hostile fire, but all indications pointed to a small defensive contingent.

Nonetheless, the scale of the defense had nothing to do with the potential peril it held for these men. However large or small the enemy might be in number, a bullet is a bullet. It comes from a single gun into the innards of a single man.

One of humans' greatest fears is fear of the unknown. It feeds upon itself, breeding more fear and associated anxiety. And with anxiety comes a disquietude that can undermine one's rational thinking.

It was unknown if the Viet Cong and perhaps North Vietnamese would resist the assault. Intelligence declared it could go either way. The best guess? Charlie would deploy snipers, hidden in the jungle and buildings in the beach city to bring down the Marines as they disembarked from the boats. Think of D-Day but on a smaller scale.

Even before climbing down the rope ladder from the transport ship into the landing craft, he recognized he was becoming scared. Not the scare of missing a free throw, the fear of missing something more important: a leg, an arm, a life.

His comrades seem composed. By the time he and 30 others were in the boat, his sweat had darkened his shirt. Running down his face, the salt from the sweat burned his eyes. His comrades' clothes and faces appeared to be dry.

The LCVP (landing craft vehicle, personnel) he was riding-in circled around for a while, allowing other boats to take on Marines. During this pre-assault protocol, he could not push the image of his father from his mind. He could not help but visualize the shell of a man his father eventually became.

Festooned with battle ribbons, his father sat catatonically on the family sofa, staring at the television screen, but not really seeing what his vacant eyes took in.

The flat-bottomed boat rode like a cork in the water. He was getting sea sick. The smell of burning fuel coupled with the erratic motion of the LCVP brought forth a wave of nausea. He was nearing panic.

He tried to stay focused: *Don't hesitate to get out of this boat when the ramp goes down. If you get shot, it will be over with. Don't let anyone know you've got the shakes.*

When a person watches another person, what is seen are unequivocal acts; clearly spoken words; unambiguous movements and gestures; indisputable facial expressions. The observer does not see the confused, muddled thoughts that went into the creation of those clear-cut performances.

The observer concludes it is only he who suffers from these mental reservations.

With some exceptions, the men in the landing boat were going through similar psychological dramas and traumas to that of the football hero. If he were able to peer into their minds, he would have been greatly relieved to know he was not the odd man out. But he could not peer into their minds. He could not know of their fear. He lived in his own skin, not the skin of others.

Several LCVPs had now formed the first assault wave. Side by side, they gathered speed. Churning along at an excruciatingly slow nine knots, he felt compelled to shout to the coxswain who was steering the boat, *Are you mad going this slow? We're sitting ducks out here!* But the boat could not make more speed.

Minutes passed by, time seemed to be suspended. The son's dread of the opening of the bow ramp on the beach fed his fear. He was holding on, but close to losing his nerves and going to pieces.

The first wave of LCVPs finally made their way to the beach. What awaited him when the bow ramp went down? A bullet into his body? A shell exploding around his head? Nothing? He raised himself from a squatting position, and pushed his way from the stern of the boat to the bow.

Taking action against that which is feared can be a way to assuage the fear itself. By moving to the front of the boat, he had decided to get it over with—whatever *it* might be. Fear feeds on inaction. If he were going to get shot, it might as well happen a few seconds sooner. What's a few seconds when the mind has almost shut down anyway?

The landing craft rode the surf to the beach. To stabilize the boat, the coxswain gunned the motor to move the flat bottom onto as much sand as possible. The bow ramp went down. The man lunged forward, passing over the flat ramp in two steps. He ran into shallow water with his head lowered.

Once on solid sand and past the surf, he looked up to find a place for cover. There, he found himself looking at a smiling woman. She approached him and placed a lei around his neck. He turned to see that several Vietnamese women had come to the beach to welcome the United States into the Vietnam War.

For now, the Viet Cong would wait it out. For now, he was grateful to Charlie. He had made the first step toward his goal. He hoped none of his battle mates saw in him what he thought was mental reactions that were close to cowardice. His battle mates were hoping the same as he. None of them knew they were all in the same boat in more ways than one.

CHAPTER 9

SYLVESTER CROSSES
THE FINISH LINE

The time was a fall morning in the early 1950s. The location was a high school football locker room in a small southern community. The room was occupied by twenty-five boys. Twenty-four were white. One was black. The black boy was named Sylvester.

Sylvester had ventured into a black man's no-man land. In theory, the town's schools and businesses were integrated. After all, desegregation orders had been handed down from the nation's capital: All aspects of the town were to be integrated. White with black, black with white, all in accordance with the laws of America.

The orders were overdue by many decades. But truth spoke to reality. Few blacks had the nerve to enroll in the whites' schools, and fewer had the courage to enter a white store.

For this story, the focus is on a football locker room. An air of enmity pervaded the space. After all, it was a white-only sanctuary. None of these white boys had ever considered having a black in their lair. Yet, here he was. As the white boys said: "Can you believe this? We've got a nigger from across the tracks trying out for our football team. Shit! He might even use our showers."

Sylvester was skating on thin ice. The blacks were confined to their small community across the railroad tracks. There, they had a couple stores and practically no schools. Most of the blacks in what many whites in the community called nigger town could barely read or write. Those who were literate were largely self-educated by their parents or had been tutored by local church members.

The roads on the white side of the tracks were mostly paved, even the one road leading to the black semi-ghetto. The road was covered with asphalt up to the railroad tracks. On the other side of the rails, the road resembled the dirt street found in a third world country.

Those blacks who worked on the white side of the tracks had to walk through white neighborhoods to reach their place of employment. If they kept their heads down, they usually avoided confrontations or verbal belittlement. The whites knew the blacks were on their way to servitude at a white's enclave and usually left them alone…if they kept their heads down. Looking around too much, and especially looking at a white woman, was not a prudent practice. Blacks had been lynched for making such a glance.

On this day, when Sylvester made his way from his home to the football facility, he encountered a typical racial slur, "Hey look, there's a nigger in our wood pile!"

Head down, he kept walking. He was used to these insults. They had nothing to do with him. They had to do with those who spoke them. Sylvester knew himself and was proud of this understanding. Those around him had no idea of his resolve and determination to make his way in life.

Jobs for the blacks in this town were menial. At the top of the hierarchy of the few well-to-do blacks were the bootleggers. After midnight, the bars on the white side of the tracks were closed. The heavier drinkers had not consumed enough alcohol to fortify themselves against a soon to be rising sun. The answer was the black bootlegger from across the tracks. He was open 24 hours a day, even on Sundays.

Double the price for a case of beer? It made no difference to the drunks. Their wallets took care of this trivial overhead. Venture across the tracks after midnight? It made no difference to the whites. Their skin color gave them a suit of armor against any potential violence. A black man and his community would risk deadly retaliation if a white was harmed in black town.

Racism had been litigated away in Washington. Try telling that to the residents who lived on the other side of the tracks. Then why was Sylvester suiting out in a white's-only locker room? No black had ever set foot in the place. Why had he walked across the tracks this fall morning? Why had he bothered to be the butt of more racist insults?

Was Sylvester's action the result of coincidence or irony? Irony implied causation between events. Coincidence did not.

On the wall of Sylvester's home was a fading, curled photograph. It was made in the late 1800s. In the picture was his great grandfather, along with Theodore Roosevelt and other soldiers of the Spanish-American War battles in Cuba. The future U.S. President had posed for several photos after these fights. Most of the pictures showed only white soldiers standing with their commander. A few photographers had kept a few black faces in their images...perhaps by accident.

Sylvester did not see it this way. He believed Roosevelt wanted to be pictured with black soldiers. Beneath the photograph was an equally aged note, a quote from a speech Roosevelt had made about the black soldier.

Sylvester had memorized the quote: "It was my good fortune at Santiago to serve beside colored troops. A man who is good enough to shed his blood for the country is good enough to be given a square deal afterward."

Coincidence or irony? It did not matter to Sylvester. He had a former United States President behind his back. Besides, he was faster than greased lightning, and he knew it. He had something to show: his God-given speed. He had something to prove to himself, to the whites living across the tracks, and to his great grandfather.

Once again, theory is one thing, reality another. Racist innuendoes and sometimes less-than-veiled threats permeated the locker room. They carried their way onto the practice field. *We're going to knock that asshole's black ass into the ground. We're going to dropkick that nigger back to nigger town. He ain't staying in this locker room for long.*

For the first hour of this first day of training, the boys were taken through routine warm-ups and drills that most of them had mastered the year before. Sylvester was a black babe in the woods of whites. He had no experience with football calisthenics, but they were easily taken on. Next came the sprint drills. Sylvester had considerable experience with running. It was one of his favorite ways to spend his time. No one in his neighborhood came close to matching him in speed.

But what about the whites across the tracks? He had never raced against a white boy. True, he kept President Roosevelt's praises for his race and his great grandfather in mind, but if the coloreds were so gifted, why were they confined to dirt roads and run-down homes across the tracks? These questions had lingered in his mind for many years.

He put these questions aside for the moment. He had come across the tracks to concentrate—in a modest way—on living up to what his great grandfather had done.

Thus, it was a fall morning in a small community in the south that Sylvester took on a new status in the white and black communities. And with that status, he would further solidify his dignity and, ever so slightly, raise the dignity of the inhabitants on his side of the tracks.

In platoons (teams) of five each, the boys lined up for a one-hundred yard sprint. The winner of the five-boy race would later race against the winner of the other four sprints. This drill was one of importance for all the players. Whether a lineman or a runner, speed is essential to success on the gridiron. For a receiver or a running back, speed outweighs size.

Sylvester, who wisely felt out of place in white neighborhoods and white locker rooms, was now in his element. Let the races begin!

His race was the third of the five races. He glided to a ten-yard margin win. He eased up on this sprint, knowing he had another race to run that morning.

The five winners of the previous sprints lined up at the zero yard line. They had one-hundred yards to go to gain a significant place on the team and in the community. They knew they were not just running a race. They were vying for the title of the fastest man on the team and the fastest five-man team on the football squad. The times of the five runners on each team were added-up to yield a "team" score. Both titles conveyed honors, which gave them inroads into the coaches' playbook for standout plays and the titles of the fastest boy and racing team in town.

Before Sylvester left his house that morning, he looked once again at the faded photograph and the note on the wall.

My ancestor went all the way to Cuba. All I have to do is walk across whitey's town and run on his football field.

The final race stunned the entire assemblage, including sidelined plodders, Sylvester's four competitors, as well as the coaches. Sylvester scorched the other runners. The nearest contestant was over ten yards behind Sylvester when he crossed the goal line at the other end of the field.

But Sylvester was not immune to some slurs that could be heard from the sidelines. "Run, nigger, run!" stayed in his mind.

Astonished by the boy's athleticism, the idea of a winning team built around Sylvester began to take hold. A football championship was the stuff of dreams for many American towns. And indeed, Sylvester lead the team to a state championship in their division.

Sylvester was now more-or-less accepted into the locker room, where racial mutterings were muted by his feats. He walked the streets on the white side of the tracks with less fear than in the past. Winning a state championship in a football-crazed town did wonders to mask racism. The town basked in its football glory. If the glory came from black legs, that was the price the town was willing to pay for its bragging rights in the state.

The stark reality of this surreal environment was not confined to this one town. It was identical to thousands of other communities across the country—an almost indigenous characteristic of American culture.

Nonetheless, because Sylvester now crossed goal lines and his team ran up their scores against their opponents, he could finally cross the tracks into whitey's closed society without trepidation. Before football season had started, he could have hardly imagined walking down an American street without fear of scorn, perhaps retribution, from white citizens.

This is not to say other black people in this community were bequeathed this privilege. But Sylvester was. After all, his picture appeared in the local paper. The white folks knew him. They understood he brought the town a rare gift: a state football championship.

In the state championship game, Sylvester broke free from the line, eluded the linebackers and cornerbacks, and headed for a touchdown. The white fans in the stands shouted, "Run, Sylvester, run!"

CHAPTER 10

AN OIL BATH

O il field work was one of the most highly paid blue collar occupations in America. It offered big salaries for certain jobs, some that required a modicum of skill and tenacity. For some duties, the activities were risky. Coming from many walks of life, the oil drilling rigs attracted workers of varying skills and diverse views on how they went about living.

Regardless of their nature and status within their loosely formed associations, they were as varied as any working class population. The men on the rigs were called *roughnecks* by the locals. The roughnecks at the top of the drilling rig hierarchy were the *drillers*. They were in charge of the crew on the rig during their working shifts.

The low man on the totem pole of roughnecks was the *roustabout*. He was usually a drifter, an oil field vagabond and was not allowed to work on the drilling rig itself. Often reeking of vodka from the previous night, these individuals could not be counted on to show up for a morning's shift.

However semi-drunk, many of his kind made their appearance at an oil company office/garage on the outskirts of town. In the early morning hour of 6 am, it made little difference if a man was still staggering a bit in the small crowd of equally inept discards from humanity.

Yet his unskilled labor was an important part of oil well operations. However mentally disassembled he may have been, his work was needed in the oil field.

The roustabout's duties were varied. He painted. He assembled and disabled pipe parts.

With a shovel and hoe, he maintained the sides of the dirt oil pits around the drilling rig. These ponds contained the disposal of drilling debris, such as mud and cuttings from the drilling rig. Their foul contents seeped into the surrounding landscape and into the earth beneath it.

The role of the roustabout was dirty and degrading. But he had rolled his own dice. Had he made even half-hearted attempts to improve his skills—including for some, staying off the bottle—he could be working on the drilling rig itself, earning good money and laboring in a more prideful position.

One of the more onerous and dangerous tasks in an oil field was cleaning the insides of large crude-oil tanks; not the sides of the tanks but the bottoms. A near empty tank still contained a thick layer of oil sludge, which had to be pushed and pulled (swept) toward a door at the side of the lower part of the tank. There, the normally sealed door would be opened where the roustabouts would sweep and shovel the remaining oil into barrels sitting outside the tank.

Because of the toxic fumes emanating from the sludge, all tank cleaners were instructed not to enter the tank, but to stand outside the tank and employ rubber scrappers attached to extended handles to guide the sludge to the door as best they could. It was a nearly impossible task as the tanks (and their bottoms) were huge. For a proper cleaning, going into the tank—for a short time—was an untold part of the job.

Due to the reputation of roustabouts, as well as the non-steady work they performed, they were hired on a daily basis. Each morning, a motley group of men, mostly hung over, assembled in front of the headquarters of the drilling company. The night before, the boss of the overall drillers had decided which rigs needed repair, which pits needed maintenance, which pipe batteries and rigs were to be assembled or disassembled, and which oil tanks were to be cleared of sludge.

The men stood in front of the headquarters, hoping to be selected for the upcoming day of work, to gain some money for their dinner and next bottle of booze. They waited for their names to be called from the list they had recently signed. If selected, with relief, they stepped onto the bed of a truck that would ferry them to their worksite. Ten hours later, the truck would pick them up and take them back to the headquarters. There, they would be paid in cash to tide them over to the next day—where they might or might not show up.

In the crowd one morning was a rookie roustabout. He was unemployed and nearly broke. His skills were minor—having dropped out of college, and looking for a way to gain a grip on the slipping away of his early twenties. He had heard about the happenstance hiring of similarly unskilled workers at the drilling office. He had nothing to lose. The next day, he put his name on the list for a day of roustabouting.

"Frank Simms?" yelled the hiring manager.

"Yes, sir!" yelled the college dropout.

"It says here, you had a summer of doodlebug [prospecting] experience: setting dynamite holes?"

"Yes, sir. Last year."

"It says you have a year at college."

"Yes sir. But no more money for school."

"And you hope to earn it here?"

"Gotta start somewhere, sir."

"Well, look at this boys! We got a college man in our ranks! Mr. Simms, I'll take you on today. You'll go with Smitty to clean out those tanks in area 24. Smitty will show you the ropes."

There was a diffused mummer in the crowd. Smitty occasionally showed up for the 6 am roll call. He was usually half drunk and, consequently, was left out of the work crew for that day. At one time, the man had an elevated status among an admittedly low level of contestants. But the booze got to him. His attitude and spirit experienced a similar decline. Smitty was going through the motions of living but not doing a very good job at it.

The man's nature involved not much talking, incessant smoking, and terse answers; mostly silence, surrounded with an aura of animosity. He and Frank formed a dysfunctional combination, courtesy of a semi-literate envious hiring manager who dismissed them onto the truck bed with his thoughts: *A college boy and a drunk reprobate. They deserve each other.*

Cleaning a nearly empty oil tank was not a labor of love or an exercise in rocket science. These operations are now more automated. But in the days of this story, for the older tanks, the men pulled the sludge next to the door, where they shoveled it into the barrels, then laboriously careened the barrels away from the tank to await their removal by a lift and truck. Still, this procedure kept them out of the tank.

Smitty defied logic, as well as intelligence. He waded into the tank and began pushing the sludge toward the tank door. "Hell fire, let's get this done, so we can rest a while."

Frank was breathing in the oil fumes from even outside the door. "Smitty, you're crazy. No way I'm going inside that tank."

"Suit yourself. Just shovel this shit into the barrels as I push it to the door."

In confusion and disgust, Frank walked away from the tank and sat down. There, he remained for a minute or so until he heard a muted splash inside the tank. Fearing for the worst, which is what happened, he ran to the door. There, he discovered Smitty lying face-down in the sludge. The fumes had gotten to him.

Taking a deep breath, Frank waded-in, grabbed Smitty by his shirt, and pulled him out of the tank. The victim was breathing but only half-conscious. Frank kept him lying on his stomach while he rigorously pumped his back.

Gradually, the oil laden man, reeking with sludge, began to come around. Who could know which was slurring his speech, the fumes from the oil, or the alcohol from the vodka. Probably both.

In gratitude to Frank for saving his life, Smitty offered, "My smokes are soaked with oil. Better not light'um up. ... Gotta cigarette?"

CHAPTER 11

FRANK'S FARMACY

This story is full of facts. Not alternative facts but facts. The setting for this fact-filled story is a drugstore. Keep in mind during this report that the name "drugstore" is a factual fact, but the name drugstore can no longer be used. It's an unfactual fact. Why? Because it contains the word "drug." The problem is that a druggist can no longer sell drugs. He must sell pharmaceuticals.

Nor can he be called a "druggist," as that term is associated illegal narcotics dealers. He can be called a prescriptionist or a pharmacist. And behind his pharmaceutical counter, shelf-after-shelf—resting tranquilly—are dozens of the most powerful tranquility inducing drugs in existence.

"Hey, ma, I've got this prescription to buy some opioids."

"No way! You are not allowed in drugstores. They sell *drugs*."

"Okay, I'm headed down to the street corner to buy some opioids."

"That's a different story. Bring back a few pills for your dear old mother."

In the interest of non-relevant facts, I have digressed, as our story is about a specific drug…that is, pharmacy store. This establishment suffered from numerous handicaps.

First, it was an old store. It even had an antiquated soda fountain located next to the pharmacist's counter. It was housed in an even older building within a city in the south-west near the Mexican border.

Second, it was locally owned, not part of a chain, which allowed the giant "drugstores" to offer discounts on their wares, such as toys, tires, radios, cameras, milk, clothes, beer and liquor. On the side, these stores sold a few bottles of medicine.

Third, the owner was from the old school. His small business offered personal service for each customer who walked though its doors, while the larger competitors' huge inventory precluded this kind of care. Shopping in these big stores was akin to searching in a lost-and-found locker—a giant locker. The philosophy of the chain stores: Let the customers wander around looking for their needle in a haystack. More often than not, they would find additional needles for their shopping baskets—which was the intent of the serviceless operations of the big stores in the first place.

Not for the hero store of this saga. The owner was proud of his store's attention to his customers. A sign on his front door proclaimed, "Service First, Service Second, Service at all Times!" A truthful yet expensive proclamation, as personal service added considerable overhead to the small store.

Fourth, being small, it could not offer the variety of selections of its larger competitors. As an example, the owner could not afford to stock his shelves with Safeway grocery products. But the big pharmacies could and were prime competitors with the grocery store chains.

Fifth, its owner was a Mexican. Brown-skinned folks were not looked upon fondly by the surrounding white-skinned neighbors.

Sixth, the age-old soda fountain did not bring in many customers. It had no booths or high-backed chairs. Fifteen stools were bolted into the floor next to a Formica counter. A part-time cook prepared an order from scratch—far too long for its Twitter population to wait to eat what was actually a meal.

The future did not look bright for this small business. It was being overrun by the big box stores. But the darkest clouds do not stay dark, because the neighborhood was also being overrun by Latinos. Hundreds of brown-skinned people were flooding into the city from the south.

The store owner (its only pharmacist), in an attempt to populate his nearly deserted soda fountain and prescription counter finally decided in desperation to place advertisements in the local newspaper about the virtues of the pharmacy's soda fountain. They read: AT FRANK'S FARMACY, HAVE A FREE COKE WHILE WAITING FOR YOUR PRESCRIPTION TO BE FILLED!

These ads were a good idea, even if Frank was named Jose. It made no sense to pay for negative advertising by using his real name. Jose knew the neighborhood; thus, it was best the neighborhood did not know him as Jose. The name of Jose's Pharmacy would be akin to a reverse end of a magnet, pushing potential patrons away.

Shrewd marketing, but the tide kept running against Jose's small enterprise. Nonetheless, some prescription customers began to come to the small cafe for their free soda. A few customers even ordered ice cream or a milkshake, some a sandwich. Temptations exist everywhere, at drug counters, even soda fountains.

During these difficult times, Jose had an epiphany. He came to realize the money-losing soda fountain offered an advantage over his rivals. The other pharmacies did not have this facility or the space to install one.

Taking advantage of the situation, Jose took out other ads in the local paper to proclaim: FRANK'S FARMACY: FREE COKES WITH YOUR PRESCRIPTION. FRANK'S ALSO SERVES FRANKS! AT A DEEP DISCOUNT WITH A PRESCRIPTION PURCHASE!

Walgreen's and Rite Aid had no counter-punch. While they sold pills, and merchandise that competed with local grocery stores, Best Buy electronics, hardware stores, and clothing shops, they had no soda fountain.

* * *

Latinos were close to overcoming the number of whites in the city. Everywhere Jose went, he saw as many brown-skins as he saw whites. Times were changing. Frank discerned this fact in his pocketbook. Increasingly, his income was coming from Latinos.

For the few soda fountain customers, browns had even taken over the stools during lunch. Hamburgers were not bigoted as to who ate them. Of course, Mexicans eating at the small counter further distanced the white folks from Frank's Farmacy.

The pharmacist was certain he was correct about the racial and cultural changes taking place in this part of town. In anticipation of the consequences of these changes—a mark of wisdom on the part of Jose—he sent a part-time employee on a scouting mission of the two competing, nearby pharmacies. At the stores, the boy was to meander around their aisles, all the while counting the number of white and brown customers. He reported back to his boss:

"Just about all white, sir. I came across three Latinos in one of the stores. They seemed confused about the shelf medicine and were talking with one another in Spanish and shaking their heads about their problems. No one in the store offered to help them…seemed to want to avoid them. I approached them and told them in my broken Spanish about your pharmacy, that they could get free advice in Spanish and still buy nothing, but if they filled a prescription there, they would get free Cokes and cheap hotdogs while they waited for their prescription to be filled.

"…There they are now, coming through the door!"

"Good job! Did you spot any more Mexicans?"

"Two in the other store. I told them about your pharmacy and the free cokes if they filled a prescription. I got chased out of the second pharmacy by a security guard. So did the Mexicans."

Even though he was losing the whites, Jose (Frank) was gradually cornering the growing market for Latinos. They liked conversing with a pharmacist in Spanish. They appreciated that Jose's few employees actually attempted to assist them.

The suburban area around the three pharmacies continued its rapid growth. The minorities now included migrants from Asia. They and the Latinos were displacing white families, who were fleeing to their closed gate communities located in a more acceptable part of town.

The time was ripe: Frank launched a new marketing campaign in the local paper. He ran a short TV commercial. One caption in the ads proclaimed: FRANK'S FARMACY: FIT FOR FINE FOREIGNERS! It was a risky sales ploy, but it paid off.

After losing substantial business to Frank's, one of the other pharmacies eventually closed its doors. Jose hired a bilingual pharmacist. As an additional nail in his competitor's coffin, Jose added tacos to the soda fountain menu.

He changed the sign on the front door of the store: "¡Servicio primero, servicio segundo, servicio en todo momento!"

Which brings us to the end of this saga. Whatever it may be, Trumpian semi-facts or Trumpian alternative facts, the story about Jose and his store represents what has happened in many American communities; beginning a few decades ago and is still happening today…Trump's Wall notwithstanding.

This old saying describes Jose, "Wisdom is knowing what to do next; virtue is doing it."

CHAPTER 12

WIRE TRANSFER

"Hello."

"Is this John Rawlings?"

"Yes, who is this? Hm, you sound familiar. Is this Luigi Diago?"

"It is. You've a good memory, John."

"Ha. Same voice, Luigi, even after...say, how long has it been? Twenty years or so?"

"Yep, twenty years ago. We last saw each other the week I was headed for the Marines. You were in town from college visiting your folks."

"I remember. I came over to your parent's house. After high school, we kept missing each other. Me in one town, you in another. I met your wife and son that day. He was a little tyke; four or five...and sing, all he did was sing. Could he ever belt-it-out! He had your genes, Luigi, a baby Caruso."

"Yeah, he still sings beautifully. You probably don't remember, we named him Mario...you know, after Mario Lanza. He's making some money here and there with his voice. He has a part time job to keep him singing. I'm very proud of him."

"Luigi, I lost track. Did you continue singing? Do you still sing? You were the star of our town. People came to our Sunday church sessions just to hear you sing. I recall our First Baptist Church, Reverend Vowell, joking to the congregation that Luigi Diago was drawing in Methodists from across the street to listen to your Baptist hymns. That got a lot of laughs, except for the Methodists in the pews."

"I'd forgotten about those times. Now, it seems so far away."

"I recall your doing those solos, all without music in the background. That is what stunned us listeners, Luigi. No instruments, no other singers. You didn't need them. I can still hear your songs in my mind. I didn't say anything about it in those days, but your voice was mesmerizing."

"Thank you, John. At this point in my life, your comments mean a lot. By the way, it's called a cappella. I kept singing and became part of the United States Marine Corps Band, even sang solos at quite a few Marine concerts. We often toured across America. On most of the concerts I did a solo. My dreams of singing, of performing, had come true.

"But eventually, the old voice box couldn't keep up. I finally had to give it up for a desk job. Not what I had in mind for my career."

"Sorry, Luigi. I've had my share of bad breaks, too. But here we are! Middle aged, and still ticking. And it's good to hear from you. Your call has really surprised me."

"I'm glad I reached you. ...John, I need a favor."

"Name it."

"You probably don't remember, but the last time we saw each other—before the Marines—I borrowed twenty dollars from you. Hadn't yet drawn any military pay."

"I have no recollection of that loan, Luigi. What a memory. Forget it."

"No, a debt's a debt. I'm paying you back. But for now, I'm in the same situation as I was back then. I've got a pay check problem. I'm out of the Marines, discharged last week. I had back pay coming, but I couldn't draw on it."

"I was paid in full the day I mustered out of the army. What happened?"

"My paperwork was misplaced, so I need a few dollars to keep me going a couple weeks. I'll get the back-pay and some disability money and repay both loans."

"Disability? You're on disability, Luigi?"

"It's a long story, John. Next time we see each other, I'll buy you dinner and fill you in."

"Okay, Luigi. How much do you need?"

"Could you spare two-hundred dollars for a couple weeks?"

"Of course. How do I get it to you?"

"I need it soon, John. I'm at the local Western Union office in our hometown. Can you wire it to me today?"

"There are several Western Union offices up here. I'll have one of them wire the cash today. Shouldn't take long. … Disability. Are you going to be okay?"

"Just need some breathing space to collect myself. I'll be fine with a little time and some military checks coming in. I hated to call you, John. I started to call Mario, but he's strapped for cash, and half-worried to death about my disability."

"No, you did right by calling me. By the way, that twenty year-old twenty-dollar loan's been accruing interest. We'll keep it simple. When your military checks start coming in, just counter-sign 'em and pass on to me!"

"I really do owe you interest on that loan, John. But I have no idea what it is."

"I was joking. I don't know either and care less. I'm glad to help an old friend. Who knows? I could easily be the one calling you one of these days. I'm on my way out the door to do the wire transfer, Luigi. You'll have the cash very soon."

"Thank you again, John. God, I hate doing this."

"It's not your fault, Luigi. Who has control over their disabilities? I'm drawing VA disability because my own government sprayed me with Agent Orange. Don't blame yourself, just makes things worse. Things will work out. Just like my Agent Orange checks, yours will start coming in. I know you don't want to talk about it now. Maybe later, after you're settled. So long for now. I've got to get moving."

"Thanks, and goodbye, John."

* * *

"Hello."

"Is this John Rawlings?"

"It is. Who is this?"

"My name is Mario Diago, Luigi Diago's son."

"Mario! I haven't seen you since you were almost a baby. What a coincidence. I just spoke with your dad a couple days ago."

"Yes, I know."

"Oh, how so?"

"Found some paperwork in my dad's motel room. One piece of paper showed a wire transfer for two-hundred dollars. On the back of the paper was a hand-written note from dad. I'll read it to you, 'Owe John two-hundred twenty dollars, plus interest.'"

"The so-called interest was a joke between us. ...What's going on, Mario? Why are you calling?"

"The motel maid found dad dead this morning. He drank himself to death. Empty bottles everywhere. Police called the next of kin: me. Looks like he drank up his discharge money, then apparently called you."

"Two-hundred dollars of booze?"

"He had some money left over, thanks to you. It was scattered on a table and in his wallet. Haven't bothered to count it."

"Died from alcohol? I didn't know Luigi drank, much less to excess. As high school buddies, we never had a drink, not even a beer."

"Well, he obviously did drink, and a lot. Truth be told, he lost his voice to booze. Couldn't even sing in a church choir, one of his favorite things to do. After twenty years and eligible for retirement, he was cashiered out of the Marines."

"I'm at a loss for words, Mario. I'm so sorry. Please let me know if there is anything I can do. Let me know of any funeral arrangements. I'll be there."

"No, don't bother. You did quite enough to my father with your wire transfer."

That was the last conversation John Rawlings had with any member of Luigi Diago's family.

CHAPTER 13

OVERDUE ACCOUNT

James was hired but not before the finance company's collections department expressed reservations about his qualifications. His problems were two-fold: too young and too white. He would be working in a suburb within an American east coast metropolis. It was a downtrodden, trash-strewn part of the city populated by many welfare African Americans with a few Latinos mixed in. James' job title was a field collection agent, more commonly known as a bill collector.

The city was not known for its inhabitants being fond of white people or bill collectors, much less white bill collectors. The company's collections department incessantly pleaded with the personnel department to hire seasoned bill collectors who were black. A white man who dunned blacks was asking for trouble.

It was a dangerous job. Bill collectors were often assaulted by their customers. In some situations, they were taken to a hospital as a result of their soliciting payments for a debt.

While rare, on occasion they were killed, usually not at the location of the debt dunning. They were murdered later on the streets of the ghetto when the bill collector accidently came across the customers he called deadbeats.

Ghetto debt collectors had their pride, not to mention their lucrative commissions for collecting overdue debts and repossessing debt ridden cars. An aggressive field agent could make a fine income from the company's errant customers.

But agent turnover was high. Black agents often walked off the job or had been fired for not repossessing enough cars or furniture or for not collecting overdue accounts. The wages and possible bonuses were not worth dissing their brothers. They lived in the same city and learned that hounding their urban neighbors for past due bills was not in their long term interests.

Furthermore, they did not like to collect from a bro and hand it over to a cracker company whose managers were white. The offshoot to this situation was the near absence of making collections by some of the black bill collectors; not all, but a significant number. Perhaps coincidentally, but more to the truth of the matter, these unsuccessful bill collectors remained in one piece while living in the neighborhood.

The personnel department of the loan shark company where James had recently signed a contract decided to take a new approach. They would place on the street only agents who lived outside the ghetto, agents who had no stake there; no relatives, no friends, no "brothers," no easy touch.

James was hired because his presence was better than having no one in his soon-to-be-assigned territory of collecting overdue bills. The company had its reputation to maintain: *Get our money back! If not the money, then the car or furniture.*

The company's management adapted the practice of hiring white bill collectors living outside the ghetto to avoid the bro-to-bro collection problem. In addition, James was white, young, lived in another part of the city, as well as being big and strong. Ideal traits for a bill collector.

By taking this job, James demonstrated he possessed another quality that was not to his advantage: naiveté. However, the company was experienced at training and handling new field collection agents. After all, there were no colleges for graduate school programs specializing in debt collection. Training was on the job, not in a class room.

The newly hired agent was thankful for the job. It offered decent pay, bonuses for keeping an account's interest up to date, more bonuses for collecting principle on the debt and especially for repossessing a vehicle. He also had a company car, which could be used during non-business hours.

The job suited his needs for the time. It would provide him a window to look for something better. How much better? He was not certain. He was a recent import to the east coast from a small town in Texas. He did not know much about urban life. He was clueless about ghetto life. The fact was that James knew little about any of the ropes of life.

He spent the first week in training by getting to know other ropes: the ropes of collecting overdue bills and repossessing cars and furniture. He rode with a man known as the "bad ass mother," a grizzled man who was given this moniker by office personnel.

Bad ass was both a complimentary and derogatory phrase. It was one of admiration when applied to a white agent by another white. It also described the company's customers who not only refused to honor a loan contract, but who could be dangerous, even by the standards of the ghetto.

For this field agent, his moniker was shortened to BAD in appreciation of his collection skills and his flair for staying healthy while subjugating his pathetic clients. BAD was white and made it a point to live in another part of the city.

Upon BAD looking over James and his papers, he asked, "What gives? Why are you here?"

"I needed a job. It's that simple. I'm a psych major at school, have two more years to go, but I ran out of money, and I'm in debt. I'll work a while and head back for a degree."

"Psychology major? No wonder you're working here, you're almost unemployable.

"I've been at this job for years. I stay with it. The pay's good if you can collar enough deadbeats. They're slicker than a greased pig. They hide their cars at night so we can't find 'em.

"Anyway, I get the use of a company car. I go out at night, getting away from the missus. She's a pain in the ass. But you? You're single, barely able to drink legally at a bar. You've got it made if you can be a hard ass with the bums you'll come across. They have a million ways to dodge your efforts. You'll see.

"I'll warn you, this is not a typical white collar college job. And if you're so hard up for money, just get a loan from your employer. Ha, joke! You couldn't pay interest on the loan. That's why you and I have a job, and that's why I stick around for fat paychecks.

"Anyway, listen to what I tell you this week. This is all the training you'll get. For starters, don't try out any of that college Freudian crap around here. And never let your guard down. This city is not a school campus. There are several places you do not visit unless you have another agent with you. We'll visit them together this week. There are a few buildings, mostly bars and crack houses, that our collection agents stay away from.

"We ain't getting hazardous duty pay, kid. We leave the cops to flush them out on occasion or just wait for them to leave. Then, we can do our work. I'll point out those places to you as we drive around your territory."

"I'd wager those places are where some of our overdue accounts hang out."

"Kid, you catch on fast. Of course, that's where a lot of them hangout. Hassle free drinking and drugs. We know it, so do they. It's a silent agreement. So, you wait for them to leave the place. Find them somewhere else. At home. At a friend's. A relative's. But not in the buildings I'll show you. They're off limits.

"But you've got a lot of leverage on these people. Your key to making a collection and bonus money is threatening them. Repossession of their car, taking away their furniture. They'll find a way to pay something if you've located their car. They'll do damned near anything not to have their car repossessed. The problem is finding where they hide the cars when they're not drivin' em. Back alleys, a buddy's garage, and you've got a wide territory to cover."

* * *

To put it mildly, the week was an eye opener for James. A new world lay before him, and what a strange one it was. He was not accustomed to a culture of malice, one in which experiencing subdued fear was part of everyday life. Of course, most people in his bill collections territory were not of ill will, nor were they evil. The majority of his customers were well meaning people who had the bad luck to be born black in a black urban ghetto.

But not all of them were victims of life's dice rolls. They knew the loan game and played it well. Using false papers and made-up references, they would secure a loan, take the money, and throw away the loan papers. Pay a bit here. Pay a bit there. Maybe mail in a few dollars to apply against the interest to keep the collection leeches off their backs. But never pay off the loan and if possible, avoid paying any principal. Get an easily obtained new identity, then use it when going to neighboring 'hoods to fleece other finance companies.

And for a vehicle, the black market thrived. Trading illegal cars around a network was akin to passing a simple driver's test. Just don't let the cops happen to stop you for a traffic infraction. Otherwise, keep the car for a while, then pass it on to others.

The nationally franchised loan corporations—strategically located in low income urban areas, were also in the fleecing business, an ironic cycle of mutual manipulation. Turnabout was fair play. Besides, for these so called deadbeats, fleecing and fraud were better than working. For the finance companies, it was easier than making an ethical living.

James began to understand this finance company was not much more than an operation founded on exploitation. He came to learn he was the last link in a collection chain, a chain designed to exploit the near helplessness of people living on the edge of poverty. Many had taken on the debt with the intent of paying it off. Nonetheless, the company applied continuous pressure to keep all loan payments current. No exceptions were made.

From a standard script, the following protocol was followed: a polite phone call was made by office personnel reminding the customer the loan payment was overdue. If this call brought forth no results, another less polite phone call informed the customer his credit rating might be affected. This second call rarely motivated the customer to make a payment. After all, the customer had come to this finance company because a loan could not be obtained elsewhere. The customer was simply unable or unwilling to make payments.

The third phone call was an outright threat. If this call was not successful, the field collection agent stepped in as the last resort. The agent ended up with a cadre of helpless, well meaning customers, as well as a population of hardcore, debt-avoiding people.

Thus, James discovered his customers fit loosely into one of two categories: Customers who would do their best to honor the contract and customers who would do their best to avoid it.

For the latter person, James was often made to look the fool. Time and again, he was stiffed: "Come back tomorrow, I'll have the money."…"He's left town, no idea where he went." …"I heard he was dead." And more than once, "Don't come around here again, white boy." After three weeks of toil, James had collected only one payment. The money was applied to the interest on a furniture loan.

James tracked this overdue account to a house of questionable repair. In it lived an elderly black woman, along with a few sticks of furniture for which the woman had taken out a loan to purchase. She asked James to give her another month to make a payment before her furniture was repossessed. Her daughter was coming to town. The debt owner wanted her daughter to have no concern about the mother's precarious financial situation. Cheap but fancy furniture was her chosen decoy.

James was tempted to engage in a Freudian fellowship: *Where is the man of the house? Can he come to your rescue?* But taking BAD's advice, he responded…somewhat, "Okay, can you give me some interest? If so, I'll come back next month and we'll figure out a way to handle the loan."

"How much do you want?"

"Hm...how much can you afford?" (Not one of BAD's approaches.)

Thus, the two of them came to an agreement. As it turns out, James came around to this woman's house every week, not to collect on a debt but to talk, to converse about her life and her neighborhood. James was more interested in this aspect of the ghetto than pursuing its citizens. But then, he was a psych major.

In the past, James and the woman had experienced no meaningful relationships with the opposite race. Their coming together was a first for both of them. The relationship was not what BAD would have recommended.

James was frustrated by his inability to snare any of his inveterate debt avoiders. He shared his discouragement with the woman. In turn, she shared her despair with what life had dealt her.

* * *

James had finally tracked-down a particularly elusive debtor. He was the number one bad ass actor on the company's files. The man was five months behind on his car loan payments, a situation that was hazardous to the community reputation of the finance company. After all, word would get out that the company and that new cracker was an easy mark.

James' boss reminded him of this poor collection record and warned him he had to do better. The case had become a sore point between James and the company. The recalcitrant customer and his car could not be traced down by James. BAD was brought in to help, all to no avail.

However, James finally had this so called customer cornered. He had found the address where the man had been hiding-out and concealing the car. For now, using techniques

BAD had taught him during their five-day training, James could secure his job.

* * *

Collections department head to the branch manager, "This new kid, James, closed our most difficult account. Even BAD couldn't do it. We got the car, forced the deadbeat into paying the principal, plus the interest and penalty fees. Amazing."

Branch manager, "Where did the bum get the money in the first place?"

Department head, "Not our concern, but probably he's part of the crack group around here."

BAD, who was also in the meeting, "Yep, I talked with my police contacts. He's on their radar. We got the money before the cops did."

Branch manager, "How did James pull this off?"

Department head, "Even more amazing. One of James' other customers, another overdue account, ratted on the deadbeat. Told James where the man could be located. It turns out that James had developed some sort of...well, a rapport with the other account—an old black woman.

"She was the aunt of the man. He had been disowned from the family for his cheating them out of their money. She was happy to give James the information he needed to snare the low-life."

Branch manager, "How much is her outstanding account?"

Department head, "Four hundred dollars."

Branch manager, "That's all? Cancel her debt! Make sure James gets *all* the penalty fees and accrued interest!"

Department head, "Sir, that's never been done before."

Branch manager, "It has now. I'm the boss of this branch. Get it done."

* * *

James made enough money on this one account to quit the company and pay the tuition for his next year in college.

It could be claimed that four hundred dollars was not a lot of money. That depends on how much money one has coming in to begin with. Now, the woman could breathe easier. She greatly enjoyed showing-off her fine living room furniture to her visiting daughter.

CHAPTER 14

FETCH

*T*he puppy was tiny, as most puppies are. This one, named Millie, was especially small, as she was a Toy Poodle. Millie weighed in at four pounds, but what she lacked in bulk, she made up in spirit and affection. Even at her young age, she had never met a human who did not become her instantaneous friend. She could not resist people, nor could they resist her.

Millie's disposition was a joy to her master. The two of them and the master's wife lived in a high rise apartment. The building was adjacent to a small park, which was the only uncluttered space around this urban area. During the summer the sparseness of open air recreational areas meant the park was a magnet for children.

The couple had bought the apartment as an investment fifteen years ago. They used it as a rental unit to supplement their income. The husband's occupation kept the couple on the road most of the time. Now that he was retired and getting along in years, they decided to settle down and move into their high rise dwelling.

Their residence was a part of an apartment complex consisting of seven high rises, each one having at least twenty floors. The complex was located in the suburbs of an east coast metropolis, near the city's downtown. Thus, it was a popular place in which to live, as the commute to the city was short and convenient.

But the scarcity of playgrounds among the high rises meant the single small park was often overcrowded. Children wished to escape the confines of their small living quarters. The park was their urban oasis; not big, but larger than their confining apartments.

Fifteen years ago, this part of the city's suburbs was populated principally by white, middle class families, usually of western European lineage. Notwithstanding this near-homogeneity, there was a sprinkling of Latinos and African Americans living in the complex.

This cultural mix pleased the couple, who enjoyed their past times in parts of the world that had ethnic and racial diversity. Both husband and wife spoke Spanish and enjoyed their Latino friends' good natured jokes about their mangling Spanish verbs.

Fifteen years later, the high rise population had become even more diverse. In addition, the prevalent populace did not consist of WASPs, Latinos, or African Americans. People of Middle East descent had become more numerous than the other ethnic groups. Their dominant presence was evident during Islamic religious services. Local police had to manage ongoing traffic as vehicles vied with Muslim worshippers driving or walking to and from the local mosque.

Using the hallway connecting the apartments on the third floor, Millie's master had been teaching his pup the run and fetch game. He would toss a small toy down the hallway and instruct Millie with a "Fetch!" to retrieve the toy and bring it back to him. The pup's reward was a pat on the head, with a "Good girl, Millie."

It took Millie only a few practices to learn the game, as well as neighbors requesting that the two animals take their game elsewhere. On occasion, Millie would bark while she ran down the hall to fetch the toy. Even though the small pup's woof was of modest volume, it was a distraction to neighbors living near the couple's apartment.

The dog's master responded to a neighbors' modest complaint about the barks with, "Yeah. My enthusiasm has gotten the best of me. Sorry, I'll find somewhere else for our playground."

Neighbor, "Why not use the park? Our building has a door on the first floor that opens to one side of the park. It's a public space, so Millie would be free to run around in it. You two can enjoy fetch out there, and my wife and I can enjoy some quiet in here!"

"Ha. I appreciate your advice. ...Let's go Millie," as the two of them headed for the stairs leading to the side door.

Stairs. A new learning experience for the pup, who had never encountered stairs in her young life. After a few moments of coaxing from the master, Millie got the idea of what she was supposed to do with the steps. Before long, master and Millie had exited the side door on the first floor and found themselves next to the park.

The man reflected, *Why didn't I think of this before? And look at the kids! Millie will have a ball with them. I'll bet some of these children have never seen or held a live dog, much less play fetch with one.* Walking into the park, the man said to his pup, "You're in for a treat, Millie. So am I. Let's do a few fetches, then you can meet some of the kids. They are already looking at you."

Of course, Millie had no idea what the man was saying, but she immediately became excited. When she beheld so many people running around the grassy meadows of the park, she tried to leap out of the arms of her master.

"Want to play with them, Millie? Okay, here you go. We can do fetch later," as the man placed the dog onto the grass of the park.

Let her rip! As Millie took off and began her foray into a bunch of newly found friends. The master grinned, *These kids will go wild. I'll bet Millie is an exotic creature to many of them.*

But something strange occurred, at least it seemed strange to Millie's master. None of the children responded to Millie's attempts to play with them. Not one of the youngsters attempted to pet the pup. Some shied away from her.

Hm, thought the man, *they probably don't know what to do with a live animal! Poor urban kids. I'll introduce Millie to them.* "Millie come!" as the pup returned to her master.

Millie and the man walked around the park attempting to engage the children and lessen their anxiety about perhaps encountering a live animal for the first time in their lives. "Hello there. This is my dog, Millie. She's very friendly, loves people. Would you like to pet her?"

No luck. Not one child would touch the pup, much less pet her. After a few of these futile gestures, a man approached Millie's master. "I've been watching you and your dog. Allow me to help you. You are wasting your time with these children."

"A bit weird, if you ask me. They must be from another planet."

"No, they are from Islamic countries here on earth. For myself, I am from Afghanistan. I work in the city at our embassy. It appears you are not familiar with Islam."

"No, but what does that have to do with these children and my dog?"

"If you look at the children's mothers, you can see they are not happy with your foisting your dog on their children."

" Foisting! What kid does not love dogs?"

"Many people who are Islamic believe dogs are dirty. Many believe the Quran forbids them to touch a dog, and certainly not to allow a dog into their home. Some who own dogs have them euthanized when Ramadan is coming around, as they believe their religion forbids them to keep a dog.

"Sorry if you think I am intervening. Just trying to save you some trouble...part of my job as a diplomat, so to speak."

"Thanks for the lesson. I wonder why these people even bother having a dog if they end up killing it for religious reasons? ...No, don't bother answering. I've heard enough, and I'll follow your advice and keep Millie away from the children."

"That would be best for everyone. Again, sorry for this intrusion."

"Not at all. I appreciate your advice. Before we part company, I would like to make an observation about your culture."

"Yes, go ahead."

"You know the disparaging remarks Americans make about Afghanistan being a country of goat herders?"

"Yes, and goats are an important part of our economy."

"During my childhood, I lived on a ranch. My family and our neighbors had goats around. They are one of the most obnoxious animals I have ever encountered. Dogs are angels compared to goats."

"And your point is?"

"Islamics shun dogs but not goats. Makes no sense."

"Of course it does. We don't keep goats inside our homes. We don't sleep with goats. Of most importance, goats provide us with milk and cheese. To many Islamics, dogs do nothing useful, but—forgive my English—shit on the floor. Anyway, as I said, I'm just trying to save you some trouble. These mothers will talk to their husbands about today. Keep trying to foster your dog on the children, and you might see these men in the park tomorrow."

"I appreciate your advice. You didn't have to help with this matter. Thanks again."

The Afghan diplomat parted company with the American man and his French dog. The man now felt differently about the park. The apartment hallway and his next door neighbors were more hospitable than the people in the park.

He spoke to the pup, "No matter, Millie. This park is as much our turf as it is anyone else's. But for now, we won't play fetch out here. I'll teach you a new command. It's called 'stay'."

CHAPTER 15

HOME IS WHERE THE HOUSE IS

The two brothers had been reading about the adventures of Mark Twain's heroes. Tom was one brother, who had named his younger brother, Huck. The younger boy knew his name was not Huck, but the two boys had taken on the names of their heroes, Tom Sawyer and Huckleberry Finn.

Similar to Twain's Tom and Huck, the two boys were not tear-up-the-town yokels. However, they sometimes got into mischief from too much idleness. On one late evening, they broke the window of a drug store while skipping rocks across a sidewalk. Shortly, they high-tailed it away from the scene of the inadvertent crime and kept the incident to themselves.

While taking on their names, the characters in this story were not replicas of those in the Mark Twain tales. First, they did not fish or go exploring local streams; nor did they paint fences. Second, the boys were kinfolk. Still, like their heroes, they were high spirited and adventuresome.

In addition, they liked Mark Twain. Mark had a long moustache and mangy hair. He liked bourbon. He was irreverent, famous, easy to read, and widely read. Plus, he made heroes of children such as the characters in this story. Mark's persona and admiration for youngsters intrigued the brothers.

He was also famous but somehow managed to stay in debt, an interesting aspect of his character to the boys. After all, if he were famous, how could he possibly need money? In contrast, their father was prosperous but not famous.

Role Models and Reading

Tom and Huck absorbed many ideas from role models, a term they learned in their school classes. One hour each week was devoted to a discussion between the teacher and the students about who should be considered role models. The boys voted for Mark Twain.

The teacher informed the students their parents were to be considered role models. But the boys did not think this way. Their parents were translucent to their lives. They were not malevolent or malicious, just vague personages giving orders to their children, then going their own way. The boys were pretty much left to themselves. They managed to take care of each other.

Tom and Huck had begun to read books outside of class because their older brother had dropped by for a visit and deposited dozens of them at their home. He told his brothers he had borrowed these books from an upscale residence on the east coast. It could have been true. The books had fancy covers and fancy pages containing fancy words. But knowing their brother, they suspected the borrowing was permanent. The older brother was once again on the lam from law enforcement.

Nonetheless, after his departure, the boys found themselves with scores of books in which they initially had little interest. But during idle times, they begin skimming, then reading the books.

The parents paid scant attention to their eldest son's gifts to the children. Nor were they aware of a conversation between the three brothers before the older brother left, skipping town, barely ahead of the police.

"I'm leaving these books for you to read…besides, they're too bulky to carry around. I hope they will keep you out of trouble and separate you from this god forsaken town. You can loan the books to your teachers if you wish. Just tell anyone who asks about them that they belong to your older brother. But *don't* lose them. They are rare editions."

Younger brothers, "Okay." They wondered, *What's a rare edition?*

"Next, open these two packages."

Tom and Huck opened two boxes and beheld scores of stamps and coins, organized in binders designed to display and protect them.

Older brother, "Will you make a promise to me? (Tom and Huck nodded yes.) While I make a trip, you two are the caretakers of my stamps and coins. The books are yours. In exchange for the books I'm giving you, you must take care of the stamps and coins. Guard them! Keep them in a safe place, and never let anyone know of their existence, especially mom and dad. I'll come by later to pick them up.

"I am entrusting them to you. We are partners to keep this secret."

Younger brothers, "Why the secret?"

"Because they're worth a lot of money—much more than the books, and as I said, I must travel lightly. Going across the Mexican border with valuable stamps and coins is not a very effective strategy for avoiding the attention of customs. You're the only people I trust to safeguard them for me."

Younger brothers' thoughts, *Wow, a new adventure! We might even be ducking the law with our brother...*as they knew of their older brother's previous brushes with men touting impressive looking badges. "Your secret is safe with us."

Older brother, "I know. That's why I'm leaving them with you."

Their brother, after a cursory goodbye to his parents, and a follow-up conspiratorial talk with his two siblings, left the household, never to be seen again.

Lacking *Playboy*, which was banned from their household, they began perusing stories in the books. They enjoyed reading something besides comic books. They began to learn about the many thorns that thrived amongst their fellow humans' rose gardens and amongst the humans themselves.

They found a hiding place for the stamps and coins. They placed them on a shelf in Huck's bedroom closet. After all, the parents would have no interest in the contents of the boxes. They had no interest in the contents of their children's bedrooms or their closets. It would be the perfect hiding place for their hero's treasure.

An intellectual pursuit, if it provides stimulation and satisfaction, often leads to the pursuit of other intellectual endeavors. It's a self feeding cycle for growth and maturation. While browsing through his older brother's library, Huck came across two books, one about stamp collecting, another about coin collecting. He enlisted Tom to jointly embark on collecting stamps and coins, their own private collection.

Their new adventure led to additional reading and research, another intellectual step forward. The books included the works of a French writer named Guy de Maupaussant. As

Huck grew older, he ended up reading all the works of this man. His favorite was "The Necklace."

Thus, Tom and Huck found themselves immersed in pursuits and hobbies well beyond their Mark Twain heroes' fence painting and fishing exploits. Their new pursuits left them with little idle time; no more devil's workshops for them.

To their surprise and amazement, their amateurish studies revealed the collections purloined by their brother did indeed contain items of considerable value. They had a treasure trove on their hands, one they guarded carefully.

This newly acquired knowledge motivated them further to keep their brother's coin and stamp collection a secret from their parents. Mom and dad were apt to confiscate the serendipitous cache for themselves—if nothing else, to avenge the ongoing illegal life of their wayward son.

Their oldest brother, known in more sophisticated circles as a white collar scam artist, was only grudgingly welcome in his parents' household. Having the books in their home presented no problem, as they did not look beyond a book's cover anyway. What a load of booty they had, located right before their parent's eyes.

Home is where it is located

The parents of Tom and Huck were unusual souls. While mingling with other people, they gave the impression they wanted to be in someone else's company. They were never content with their locale and their associated "companions," even though they chose the people whose company they tenuously kept. As Tom and Huck grew older, the parents behaved as if they wanted to be in a place in which the children were absent.

The parents had divorced when Tom and Huck were youngsters. Tom took Huck under his wing, as they jointly took turns living with their parents. A few days of the year in the summer were spent with father. Most of the time, mother cared for four children, the youngest being Tom and Huck.

One day in their early teens, their mother announced that Tom and Huck were being relocated. They were to move from the home of their mother to the home of their father. This relocation was to take place on the same day of her proclamation.

Their mom had decided it was time for her two remaining children still living at home to change residences. Not for a few days, as they were going to be with their father everyday of the year. Domestically speaking, their mom was taking herself out of the picture. Their father did not express enthusiasm about this new relationship, but after many years of pushing the children onto the mother, his guilt sealed the case for the boy's new home.

On the day of this familial divorce, off the boys went. With clothes, shoes, sports gear, and other children's ware in hand, they made many five-block trips from their former home to their new domicile.

During these five-block walks, with their belongings in their arms, they walked past neighbors, as well as friends passing by in their cars. They asked the boys, "What's going on?"

"Just taking a few things to dad's place."

"Been watching you for awhile. Seems more than a few things."

Time and again, up and down the five blocks. Time and again, queried by the residents of the small town. Time and again, embarrassed and humiliated.

No help from Dad with his pickup; no help with his car, as they made their way to live with a man they hardly knew. After a day of mimicking a human moving van, they had their goods deposited in their new home. They had become outlanders in the very town where they had lived all their lives.

Welcome Home

Tom and Huck were received with folded arms by their father. He seemed no happier than they were about the new relationship. Once a prosperous businessman, he had suffered several financial losses. He had recently sold his large home and moved into a four-room house, one he owned and had used as a rental place.

He informed his sons, "Put your things away. Here are your rooms." Tom had the luxury of a single-bed bedroom. Huck occupied the sofa in the living room. He removed his sheet, blanket, and pillow each morning, just in case company came by, which it never did. His dad and stepmother occupied a third room. The fourth room was furnished as a combination kitchen and living room.

* * *

Time passed. The boys accommodated to circumstances as best they could. Their lives fell into a disjointed rhythm. Their father put up with them, but he was rarely home. Their stepmother did her best to please Tom and Huck. She cooked their meals. She tended to their laundry. She tried to talk with them, but it was to little avail. In the boys' minds, they had been exiled from their accustomed home to an alien residence.

Why? After years of enduring the life of a single mother rearing four cantankerous boys, she had said, "Enough!" She passed Tom and Huck, with a ten-minute notice, to another place to live. With almost no warning, they had been forced to immigrate.

Huck asked Tom, "What did we do wrong?"

Tom answered, "Nothing. We just wore out our welcome."

"How did we do that?"

"By being around."

* * *

Tom was gone. Huck still lived at this father's home. He and Tom eventually made their way through a nearby state college; Tom, on an athletic scholarship; Huck, by the seat of his pants and part time jobs. Tom had graduated from college the year before and was beginning his forage into the private business world. Huck returned from college for the summer break.

Huck had finished his freshman year in college. He was tempted to enroll for the summer semester, but he was eager to spend time in his hometown and reacquaint himself with his life-long friends. In addition, he had a guaranteed job for the summer.

Completing the trip from the college town, Huck pulled into the family driveway. As he walked to the back door of his home, he thought, *Hm, dad must have traded his Chrysler New Yorker for a Chevy, but where's his pickup?* The carport, next to the garage, had been closed in with laminated siding. *What the hell?*

Huck entered the house through the kitchen. There, he heard puzzling sounds coming from the corner of the room: television! It was puzzling in that his father had never allowed television in their home while any of his children were in residence. But there it was, muted sounds of "Friday Night at the Fights."

Huck walked farther from the door into the room to behold a cadre of unfamiliar people. They were watching him and the boxing bout.

"What are you doing in my house?"

"What are you doing in ours?"

"I live here!"

"No, you don't. Except for the garage in the back of the house, we bought this property two months ago. The owner moved out."

"That's my dad. Where did he go?"

"He converted the garage and carport into his home. His wife lives there with him. You know where it is, next to the kitchen. The door to their living room is a bit large; rolls up and down, but it works." The new owner had a sense of humor. Huck was not amused.

Just a few steps away, Huck found his dad and stepmother. They were living in a small two-room apartment, which formerly housed their car, pickup, and assorted piles of tools. It already had an attached bathroom at the back of the garage. By enclosing the carport and installing a small kitchen, it became a residence.

Huck noticed his father had cut a section out of the garage door and installed an opening. Huck reflected, *At least there's no need to roll up the door to get in and out.*

Opening the semblance of a door and stepping in, he saw his father and stepmother watching television. He closed the door.

"Dad, I don't know what to say. ...What happened?"

"Ran out of money, son. Needed some income."

"But you were well off! Why didn't you phone or write about your move? I've come home to no home. "

The father remained silent.

His stepmother stepped in, "He gambled it away. Property by property. House by house. Dollar by dollar. I married your dad when he was a big man in town. Now look at us. Our bedroom is a closed-in carport, and you're standing in a garage."

Huck responded, "Yeah, so I can see. I remember the layout. Tom reconditioned a car engine where the two of you are sitting."

Huck remained astounded, "We knew nothing about your problems. You never told Tom or me much of anything, anyway. But, this?" As Huck waved his hand around the living room, the former garage.

His father responded, "Yep, this is it. And we have no room here. You'll have to find another place to live."

Still dumbfounded by the surreal situation, Huck turned around toward the improvised living room door. Reality started to sink in, "What did you do with the things I had in my room, in my closet?"

Upon leaving for college, Huck had assumed his bedroom closet would continue to be a safe haven for his long-absent brother's stamps and coins. After all, he could not recall his father ever entering his domain. His stepmother kept the room clean but did not bother with his closet.

"Didn't know you needed 'em. Thought you took everything you wanted to college."

"Goddamn, Dad! I had two stamp and coin collections in the closet. Where are they? Where are my books?"

"They might be in the attic above this room. I think I put some of your stuff up there. Don't remember for sure."

"'In the attic?' 'Might be?'" Huck was angry. But spoke no further words—what good would they do? After all, he had nothing to do with his father's fiascos. From his hero, Mark Twain, from Tom Sawyer and Huck Finn, he had learned the dignity of self-composure. He left the scene, worried, but given the circumstances, somewhat serene.

Huck climbed a ladder to enter the small attic, hoping to find his brother's collections, as well as the meager set of stamps and coins belonging to Tom and himself. Although his brother's collections were of substantial value, the worth of the brothers' modest assortments was the memories each piece brought forth about how they acquired them, about how they had cared for them with a sense of accomplishment and satisfaction.

The attic contained moldy clothes, cobwebs, and dirt. It contained no coins, stamps, or books. Its vacancy created bitter thoughts from Huck. In spite of his self-imposed composure, he lamented, *What will my brothers think? Our treasures are gone.*

* * *

The oil boom around the small town had fizzled out. Former oil field workers had packed-up and moved to other places in America, including the boyfriend of Huck's mother—the one who had replaced Huck and Tom at their former home.

Huck drove the five-block passage to his mom's home. "Hello, mom, I'm back. As you know, summer break. ...Did you know that Dad has sold our home? Moved into a garage! What is going on?"

"The town's broke, son. So is most everyone in it."

"Are you alone again?"

"Yes. He lives in Midland now."

"So, my bedroom is empty?"

"Yes, but the room is up for rent."

"I have a job for the summer. If I can have my room back, I'll take care of the rent."

"Really? Well, welcome home, son."

This reunion refutes the old saying, "You can't go home again." The quote did not come from Mark Twain, Huck's hero. It came from Thomas Wolfe, a writer of more realistic stories.

CHAPTER 16

BEAR SPRAY REPELLANT

Never argue with a fool.
An onlooker may not be able to tell the difference.
—Mark Twain

The man who came in to my store last week was downright savage looking. That was saying something, as Jeb was known about town as possessing a peaceful countenance. He was never one to display himself out of the ordinary. Of course, with claw marks on his face, he stood out. Plus, he had a look that seemed out of character with what everyone knew about him. It was one of those looks that made me think, *I've never seen that look before, but I know about it.*

I know you will be asking me what kind of look could that be, and how can I see something I do not know about? Don't start off being disagreeable before I can get my story going. I will take care of your misgivings, and if perchance my declaration of unrevealed facts about a famous product does not calm your concerns, you can question my judgment about this matter at a later time.

Jeb had just come from a walk in the woods, and he was none too happy about his walk. Before I could say, "Jeb, you've got some handsome bear claw cuts about you," he got uppity and indignant. He did not even give me a chance to pass my compliment.

In no uncertain terms, he let me know he wanted his money back on a purchase he made last week. He shoved a can of bear spray repellant toward my face and said in an adamant way, "This so called bear spray repellant does not repel bears. Look at me!"

Admittedly, Jeb's still wet bear claw impressions on his checks, forehead, nose, lips, and chin left an impression on me, as well as on him, of course. He was a sight to behold, especially with his missing ear. But a sale is a sale. No refunds are permitted at this store. Exchanges are taken but no refunds. After all, a dollar earned is a dollar never refunded.

"Well, Jeb," I responded, "The only recourse to remedy your soreness about the matter is to stay in keeping with the store policy." Of course, I did not mean the soreness of his face but the soreness of his mind. I was becoming aware, and none too soon, that it would be best not to call further attention to his lacerations.

Jeb was still upset, "And what is your store policy?"

"If customers are not satisfied with a product, we will give them another."

"Another what? A different bear spray repellant?"

"No, the same bear spray repellant. We sell only one brand."

Next thing I knew, Jeb had walked out on me. I couldn't understand why. After all, I offered him a fair exchange: a full can of bear spray repellant for an empty and bent can. I couldn't even put it on my used products discount shelf.

Before I knew it, a tourist came through the door. I recognized him from his visit a few days ago, one of those city folks who like to camp outdoors. He was bleeding something awful. His clothes were torn, gone missing were a few fingers. He had left parts of his feet somewhere else, maybe at his camp site. He declared, "That bear spray repellant almost got me killed! I want my money back."

I enquired about the matter, "How did you come to use the repellant?"

"How do you think? A bear attacked me, that's how. I was walking in the woods when a bear jumped on me. I fought him off tooth and nail, but look at the results."

I thought it best not to correct his errant figure of speech of "tooth and nail" by suggesting he fought off the grizzly "hand and foot." But it was clear he was not a happy camper, and it is not store policy to rile customers further. Especially on sensitive matters, such as proper use of the King's English.

Nonetheless, it was my duty to remind him that the warranty on the bear spray repellant product plainly stated: "This product does not cover victims of a bear attack in which the attack occurs in the woods." That got his dander up something fierce. He shouted out words that will not be repeated here, as this story is meant as bedside reading for youngsters. After his unprintable pronouncements, he questioned my logic, "What's the point of using bear spray repellant if I can't go into the woods? That's where the bears are."

I offered some advice, "Your point is well taken, but then, perhaps you should not go into the woods in the first place, because that is indeed where the bears are."

I detected his rising ire, "But you sold me bear spray repellant for the very purpose of allowing me to walk into the woods!"

As gently as possible, I lent him more counsel, "Sir, I might sell you a tube of toothpaste, but that does not necessarily mean I expect you to brush your teeth."

I was afraid he might strike me a blow, but without sufficient fingers he could not form a fist. Fortunately for me, he was missing digits on both hands.

Even better news for me and my physical condition, he left with what remained of his physical condition and exited the store without further ado.

I've another set of facts for your consideration. The day before yesterday, I was tending the store, stocking up a shelf with those plastic worms that fishermen like so much. As an aside, what self respecting fish is ever going to eat a piece of plastic? It's akin to asking us humans to eat cardboard. I even had a fisherman come in here and ask for his money back on this very product. It was my duty to inform him the store's policy was no refunds.

He responded, "What can I do? I just can't go home empty handed. My wife's already invited the neighbors over for a fish fry—to take in my fisherman's catch! But I can't use these plastic worms, as I haven't caught a fish all week."

I ventured to say that he was not a fisherman, as he had caught no fish. However, I did not offer this observation, because the store policy is to have the customer always be right. Instead, I enquired, "Sir, where have you been…eh, fishing?"

"South branch."

"Ah! The south branch fish do not go for plastic worms. They lie in the water, prey to rubber worms, just waiting for that delicious rubbery tasting bait. I'll do an exchange of the plastic worms for rubber worms. After all, we can't consider the plastic worms as having been used, can we?"

I suspect he did not appreciate my oblique reference to his non-fisherman status. And the plastic worms he returned were as good as new. He bought the rubber worms and headed back to the south branch.

For me, it was a fine exchange. Rubber worms are priced higher than plastic worms. He gladly made up the difference, and I put his recently unused plastic worms back on the shelf.

Being attuned to the local wildlife, I wiped them off with a towel to get rid of their south branch aroma.

But my recounting of the events in this report is about bears and bear spray repellant, so I will return to the facts about the subject. Early this summer, I was again tending the store, restocking the deer hunting rifle rack with more AK-47s. These guns hold 30 cartridges in their clips, just in case a hunter encounters more than one deer, as deer tend to keep company with one another. And one cannot have too many deer antlers nailed to one's living room walls.

I heard a pounding at the door.

Puzzled, I went to the entrance and granted access to a gentleman who was sporting an unusual posture. I say sporting in that he was a likely sportsman, by virtue of his patronizing a sporting goods store. The truth is, he looked a bit askew. His shoulders and arms were out of alignment, and his arms seemed pinned to his sides.

But not entirely, as his two forearms and accompanying hands were thrust forward, tenuously holding a can of bear spray repellant. Poor fellow, he needed two hands to grasp what was obviously a one-handed appliance.

The proper greeting of a customer is store policy. Thus, I offered, "Good day, sir. I noticed you were pounding at the door with your foot to gain entrance. I am glad to let you in, and here you are. How can I be of further assistance?"

Looking down at his holdings, so to speak, he remonstrated, "I was attacked by a bear! I ran away, but the beast caught up with me. He lunged to bring me down and he did. Look at me! My shoulders are broken, maybe my back. I only escaped because some hikers came by and scared the bear away from my body."

It is company policy to encourage the purchase of store

products, so I began with, "Why did you not use the bear spray repellant?"

"I did! I sprayed myself and all my clothes, even my boots. I used so much spray on myself that I emptied the contents of the can."

He looked down to his can of depleted bear spray, somehow held in between his depleted arms, an observation not lost on this store keeper—your friendly story teller. I saw another sales opportunity. It was evident he was having trouble preventing the can from dropping from his hands. Being store policy to encourage customer pride and product integrity, I lent him a hand to prevent the product from falling and rolling around ignominiously on the floor.

Nonetheless, I was obliged to explain, "Sir, the directions on the back of the can are quite clear. The bear spray is to be used on bears, not humans. After all, you are not trying to repel yourself. You are trying to repel a bear."

He was not amused by my wit, and of course, store policy is not to be witty at the expense of the customer. Thus, I quickly countered my drollness, "You have the can before you. Please take a look at the directions."

"I can't turn the can around to read them!"

"Let me help you," as I ever so gently rotated the empty container around his damaged arms and hands, such that the instructions label was face to his face.

He read the directions but was far from placated, "You mean to say, I am supposed to spray a bear only when the bear is charging me?"

"Not entirely. By spraying the air around you, the bear will likely avoid the area where you are located."

"But I move around. I hike for god's sake. That's the point of walking in the woods. The air does not accompany me. The smell is left behind."

"True, and you will remember I recommended you buy more than one can of the repellant."

"But I can't spray the air with every step I take!"

A proper and successful business is built around trust. With trust, comes dependency, "Sir, our bear spray repellant has been demonstrated to ward-off bears. Rest assured that you will be safe during your walk in the woods, but *only* if you continue spraying the air around you."

He was upset until I explained that the store sold bear spray repellant at a discount if larger quantities of the product were purchased. More cans of bear spray repellant in his backpack would do no harm and likely some good. After all, hikers stuff frivolous things in their backpacks. As one example, what's the use of carrying matches if you are not allowed to light a camp fire in a forest?

I cannot say with assurance that he was entirely pleased. To complicate matters further, he kept dropping his phone when he tried to dial 911 for an ambulance, so I once again lent him a hand...so to speak.

This summer, the store has expanded its product line. We now offer two types of bear spray repellant: one for grizzly bears and another for black bears. The directions on the back of the cans provide guidance on the use of these products:

BOLD NEW TECHNOLOGY! Our new product, Bear Spray Reincarnated, comes in two cans, one for grizzly bears, and the other for black bears. Both cans come with a revolutionary nozzle, courtesy of extensive research on mists. This revolutionary second generation nozzle came about thanks to the absence of feedback from first generation customers.

As you walk in the woods, no longer will you be fearful and required to continuously clear the air with a *paltry* mist from an out dated nozzle. Go forth boldly with a *concentrated* spurt of protection!

TWO CANS ARE TWICE AS GOOD AS ONE! Make certain you purchase both the grizzly bear and the black bear spray repellants. Product selection is important. Make sure you use the grizzly bear spray only on a grizzly. Research shows that the black bear spray infuriates a grizzly, inciting the animal to more aggressive actions. The same disclaimer applies to black bears.

DIRECTIONS! If a bear lunges at you, rest assured you have two weapons at your disposal. If the bear sports a large hump on its back and displays extraordinarily long claws—which are aimed at your throat, pull out the GRIZZLY bear spray repellant. Thus armed, you can spray away! As an added reminder, spray the bear, not yourself.

On the other hand, if the attacker appears to be without a hump on its back, whose hair is black, and has unfurled relatively short claws (that is, relative to the longer clawed grizzly), be alert! If these admittedly shorter claws are also aimed at your throat, avail yourself of the BLACK bear spray.

In either case, use liberally—and quickly—before the bear, with his 30 mile-per-hour gait, closes the few feet between him and you. Selecting the appropriate weapon is important, but so is the timing of its use.

I am pleased with this expanded product line. Recently, I have not had a single dissatisfied customer come into the store asking for a refund on our bear spray repellants.

CHAPTER 17

TUNED FOR THE TASK AT HAND

The boy's favorite tool was a pair of pliers. Each morning, after awakening and dressing, he reached over to the nightstand to retrieve his treasured appliance. Placing the pliers into his hip pocket, he was prepared for another day of chores. Throughout the day, he found innumerable ways to use the tool. Unlike a jackknife, the pliers could be used for hammering, for pulling nails from discarded lumber, for tightening bolts on windmills and other machinery. Wielding his tool, the child thought of himself as one of the ranch hands. He was confident his voluntary chores made for a better operation on the ranch.

He was proud that his father knew of his mechanical and carpentry achievements. At the end of the day, while his family was having supper, his father unfailingly asked him how things went for the boy. Today, the lad informed all present he had tightened the bolts on tractor fenders, collected strands of discarded bailing wire from the hay barn, and pulled scores of rusty nails from the lumber of a recently torn-down corral.

His older siblings, his mom and dad, and most of the hired hands at the supper table praised him for his jobs well done.

His father had long bequeathed an unwritten rule that politics and religion were not part of a meal. Weather, horses, cattle, and sheep dominated the talk during the morning, noon, and evening meals.

The only reticent participant in this mutually reinforcing ceremony was a newly arrived hired hand. He remained indifferent to the household protocols, eating his meal and dismissing himself from the table. He departed to the bunk house before the meal partakers could imbibe in a few more yarns about present and past exploits, however modest they were.

No one at the table minded if the stories were not completely accurate. As tall as they may have been, if they were short enough to connect with their own experiences, the teller of the tale had done his job. He had set the stage for the next story.

Meanwhile, the child sat at these tables, listening to fables that were likely partially true, but completely true to his view of his adult heroes. Especially his father, who had the ability to listen to these stories and at the same time, offer a few of his own.

But for the most part of the day, the hours were devoted to work.

The boy's least favorite tool for this work was a paintbrush. The family ranch, covering thousands of acres on the high plains of America's southwest, was populated with scores of wooden barns and corrals. Several hours each week, the lad painted what seemed like miles of faded red barn sidings and hundreds of posts and railings.

During the cattle branding season, he was allowed to put aside pliers and paintbrushes and take on different chores. However, to the boy's chagrin, the only tool at his disposal in the branding corral was a demeaning contraption named the dope bucket. The bucket contained a small mop and a mixture of mysterious, foul smelling liquids. After a calf had been relieved of its horns and testicles, and after it had been branded, the boy hurried over to the braying prostrate animal and sloshed the medicine onto its wounds.

By the time the branding day was over, the child's clothing, shoes, face, and hands were covered with dope. Exiting the branding corral, his father joked that his son was the best dope bucket cowboy to be found: Just look at his credentials! The compliment gave the youth the fortitude to face a painful rubbing in the tub from his mother. The next day in the branding pen, he was mentally and physically rearmed.

Another chore the boy took on during the branding season was keeping his father's knife razor sharp. On alternate days, he massaged his dad's finely honed knife blade with a whetstone to produce even more sharply whetted steel. This every other day routine was not necessary to keep the blade—as his father joked, "tuned for the task at hand." The thin soft skin of calves' testicles could do little in dulling a blade made from high quality German metal.

The routine was one of several rituals of camaraderie that took place between the father and his son: *You're my best painter of barn sidings. You're my favorite dope bucket man. I've never had anyone else make my knife so sharp.*

The current summer was to be different from past years. His father declared it was time for his son to move up in the corral's hierarchy, if only for a calf here and there. For today, using his dad's knife, the youngster would be taught how to castrate calves.

The process was straightforward. The calf, lying on its back, had its hind legs spread and held fast by a cowboy. Its head was held down by another cowboy. The lad was taught to grab one testicle at a time, cut the outer skin at the bottom of the testicle, push the testicle toward the cut, then cut behind the other end, thus removing the organ from the body. If the cuts were done cleanly, the operation was practically bloodless. The newly dethroned animal, released from the grips of humans and having no clue about its altered status among the herd, was jostled by a cowboy to make its way out of the corral.

After a few tries, the boy proudly returned to his dope bucket chores. Tomorrow, he would again be granted temporary possession of his father's prized knife to perfect his fledging skills on a few more calves.

The branding days for the season were nearing an end. Many of the several hundred calves that were to undergo this age-old practice had run the corral's gauntlet. They were grazing, as comfortably as could be expected, in nearby pastures.

After his initiation into the art of castration, the boy believed he had achieved a higher status among the cowboys in the branding corral. On that late afternoon, the corral had to be cleaned by the boy. After he had shoveled blood, shit, and horn fragments into a barrel, the child made his way to his getaway place: the hay barn. There, hundreds of hay bales waited for him to apply his skills to move them from dormant bundles of green straw into fanciful moats and castles.

His meager frame and prepubescent strength prevented him from building anything of much height. He struggled with each bale of hay, somehow coaxing it to fit properly into his architectural scheme. After the castle had been built, he rewarded himself by using his pliers to snip the two wires that held a bale of hay together. He would spread the hay on the elevated floor of his castle, creating a soft, prickly bed, resonant with the sweet smells of earth. There, secure in his secret sanctuary, he would drift into and out of sleep. He

TUNED FOR THE TASK AT HAND

would later scatter this loose hay onto the floor of the milk cow pens, resulting in nary a trace of his indulgence.

Sometimes, during these interludes, he would dream of doing battle with imaginary monsters or make believe ogres. Always the hero, he vanquished the villains, reveling in his accomplishments. For today, his ascension to wearing the calf castration crown was enough excitement. He bedded down on the soft hay and fell fast asleep. He was confident he would awake in time for washing up and to be at the supper table.

He was looking forward especially to the meal tonight. He knew gentle joshing was in store for him because of his impressive performance in the branding corral. He was eager to see the look on his father's face. For now, he fell into a deep slumber.

His sleep was interrupted by a pain so excruciating he became sick to his stomach. Attempting to find the source of the pain, he turned his head. Behind him, he could make out the face of the new hired hand. The pain did not end there. He was forced over, where his mouth was then assaulted. The assailant's secret stalking of the child had at last paid off for the predator.

For the boy, the attack brought forth bewilderment. He knew enough to know what had happened. Deep down, he understood it was not his fault. However, he also transferred the rapist's actions to his own conscience. Misdirected guilt is one of the burdens that accompany humans' pride. And with that guilt: *What would his father think of him now?*

The hired hand forced a solution to his dilemma: If the child told anyone about the rape, the man would first kill his father, and next, he would kill the boy. If the boy did not show up at the hay barn after tomorrow's brandings were done—if he stole away, the man would seek out and kill the boy's father. The pedophile said he would soon be moving on, and if the boy kept quiet, things would resort back to the way they once were.

In spite of his trauma and pain, the boy challenged the man's claim of being capable of killing his dad. No one could kill his father! He was all-powerful. But the hired hand pulled out a small .22 pistol from his pocket. It held two .22 long bullets. He told the boy he carried this tool around for occasions such as this. "You be here tomorrow, boy, or I'll kill you and your daddy."

Supper was a festive affair. The branding was coming along on schedule and nearing its end. The father congratulated his son for taking a stride forward in the manly world of cattle ranching. Around the supper table, he shared that his son handled, without fanfare, what many people considered a stomach turning operation. Except for two people at the table, laughter and smiles were exchanged by all.

After dinner, the son asked for his father's knife. The father asked why, stating his son had sharpened his knife that very morning. Why dispense with the every other day agreement?

The son appealed to his father that he would be more at ease tomorrow if the knife was as sharp as possible, keeping silent about his impending second day of fear. Without hesitation, the father agreed and gave his knife to his son.

At supper the next day, the father congratulated the son once again: The child had used the castration knife with even more skill than the day before. During this meal, it was observed that the newly hired worker was missing. The man's bunkmate mentioned that the newcomer's closet was empty and his suitcase gone.

The bunkmate shared with his supper mates that the man said he would be moving on soon, but he wondered why the man had left before the branding season was over, saying nothing to him or the other hired hands. After all, by leaving early, he had given up his branding wages.

After supper, the boy returned the knife to its owner. His father said the knife had cut cleanly that day. The son agreed. The knife had been tuned for the task at hand, a fitting tool for the trade.

CHAPTER 18

ONE'S WORST ENEMY

*T*he two officers were Ensigns, fresh out of college, and more recently, graduates of the Officer Candidate School in Newport, Rhode Island. While in different graduating classes in OCS, they ended up sharing a junior officer stateroom. They were assigned to a ship in the Asian waters that surrounded Vietnam and adjacent countries: the Indochina peninsula. Their cruising extended from the Vietnamese delta in the south, the Philippines to the east, and as far north as the coast of North Vietnam.

On a late Sunday afternoon, Bill arrived at his assigned ship. He was escorted to his quarters by a seaman, where he met his cabin mate, Ron.

Upon the seaman depositing Bill's duffel bag onto the cabin floor, Ron raised up from the chair at his small desk, where he was reading a book, "Ah, Ensign Housing, been expecting you. We're underway tomorrow. Too bad, your first port of call from here in lowly Subic Bay, Philippines, is prime real estate: Hong Kong. So, on your first cruise, you can get laid for a dollar. Curing your case of the crabs is another buck, courtesy of sick bay aboard this rust bucket we're assigned to.

"A dollar?"

"Pulling your leg about sick bay, but not so much about the whores. They actually cost a few dollars, depending on the services provided. But a visit to sickbay will fix up the crabs. Free of charge, courtesy of the U.S. Navy."

The newly arrived officer began to empty his duffle bag and allocate its contents into a few drawers and a small closet. Ron put down his book: "We're both volunteers. I saw your orders, they came through the comm. center. Personnel officer told me you have a degree from an Ivy League school. Impressive I suppose, I'm a low life state college creep. Why join the Navy with your inspiring diploma?"

Bill, "For a change of pace. Besides, I was a psych major and didn't have much interest in graduate school. Not sure what I wanted to do. The Navy was a way to take a break. And you?"

Ron, "Ha! In other words, just looking for a job and a free ride, eh? Joined the military to stay off the bread line…pretty pathetic with your credentials. Did the thought enter your mind that you signed up for an outfit whose mission is to kill?"

"Never looked at it that way. By the way, why the sarcasm? You don't know me."

Ron, "I know Ivy Leaguers. They think they're better than others. Anyway, you probably never looked at it at all. Same with most so called Ivy League patriots. 'Answer your country's call! Serve Uncle Sam! Draw in that paycheck,' which you don't need anyway."

Ron continued his diatribe, "I joined the military to fulfill the military's basic goal: killing. I can kill someone without getting thrown in jail, and I've been there more than once."

Bill responded, "Jail time is recorded on a background investigation check. How did you get the clearance required of an officer?"

"My old man's sheriff of the local county; in charge of records; wanted me out of the house; never gave my jail-time records to the Feds. Hell, he himself arrested me more than once! So, he got rid of me, and I got rid of him."

The short dialogue that had just taken place took a moment for Bill to absorb. He then responded, "No offense, but are you just trying to be funny?"

Ron, "Funny? You say a change of pace! From what! Too much college pussy? What a load of phony baggage you carry; just shows your hypocrisy. You joined the U.S. Navy to get a job from an organization whose charter is, first and foremost: killing. I know the charter. I accept it, and look forward to putting it into effect."

Bill was taken aback. But he was rapidly coming to grips with his cabin mate being ill-tempered, maybe with a few screws loose. He had studied these types of personalities in school. Certain parts of their brains did not function in the customary way. This field of study was just breaking ground, but Bill knew enough about it to be leery of Ron. Nonetheless, he was stuck with the man for an extended cruise.

Bill gave it another go, "There's a difference between us. You joined the military to kill someone. I joined the military to keep someone from killing me—or to the heart of the matter, my family or my nation.

"Ron, you picked the wrong branch of service. The Marines or the army would give you better opportunities for killing. You think being an officer will give you the latitude to kill anyone you wish?"

Ron, "Yeah, it happens all the time in a war. Look at My Lai and many others that don't make it onto the pages of

Stars and Stripes or *The New York Times*. Instead of studying Freud's id, ego, and super ego idiocy, you should have been reading-up on what the Germans and Russians did to each other and what they did to the Jews in WWII—and what the Jews are doing to the Arabs and Palestinians. The Warsaw Ghetto would have wised you up more than Freud's delusions about penis envy."

Bill was taken aback by this man's arrogance, and insulted by his comments, but he remained civil, "There's a fundamental difference between sanctioned killing during wartime, and the spontaneous action of an individual illegally murdering someone. Given your mentality, good luck on your court martial."

Bill decided to explore this man's psyche. After all, Bill was a psych major, "Why not volunteer for the air force? That way, you could drop bombs and kill more than only 'someone'."

"I tried that route, a bombardier on a B-52. No luck. Bad eyes."

Still taken aback by this man, "So, you really did join the military to kill someone?"

"Relax, you're exempt. For now, I'm out to kill a slope head, after that, a Jew. Let's get a beer before we sail."

Agreements

For the next several weeks at sea and in ports along the South China Sea, Bill listened to Ron's postulations of admiration for Karl Marx's *Das Kapital* and Mao Tse Tung's distorted version of Communism. For some aspects of this seeming anomaly from a U.S. Navy officer, Bill did not disagree.

It did not take an economist to grasp that unfettered capitalism invariably led to the non-wage earners (bankers, brokers) being able to accumulate increasing capital on the backs of ordinary workers—or as Ron called them: the "peon proletariats" of the world.

Nor did they disagree that the United States had lost an opportunity to form a relationship with Ho Chi Minh, who camouflaged his nationalism with a communistic façade. Ho was a great admirer of Thomas Jefferson and the Declaration of Independence, but the U.S. had been tied to a partnership with the French, who had committed to reassert their pre-WWII control of Indochina.

Disagreements

The two men were required to share a cabin barely large enough for them to pass by each other without sucking in their stomachs. While they frequently jostled intellectually, Bill attempted to keep their discussions non-confrontational, something akin to college debates.

That is, until Bill noticed Ron was reading *Mein Kampf*, the treatise by Adolph Hitler that formed the basis for the genocides against the Jews in mid-twentieth century.

"*Mein Kampf*, Ron?"

"Have you read it?"

"Yes, in one of my history classes. Why are you reading it now? We're involved in a different war. You should be reading Mao's rantings. He's supplying North Vietnam with supplies and money. The Ho Chi Minh opportunity was lost and is history. Study Mao. He's an egotistical sadist."

Ron, "My kind of man! I read his *Little Red Book*. I like his philosophy. It fits in with mine. Essentially, fuck everyone but the Communist party, just like my hero, Joe Stalin."

Ron continues, "Bill, you're blinded by your ignorance. Jews are destroying America. Look what they're doing in

Hollywood. Every other movie is about Jews and their suffering. For god's sake, who hasn't suffered in our world at one time or another?"

And continues, "Look what the Zionists are doing in Israel. They're creating a Hitler-form of genocide against the inhabitants of that land. They're no better than the European imperialists in the eighteenth century who subjugated most of the world's nations."

Bill remained, as best he could, unemotional and analytical, "But the book you are reading led to massive genocide, ethnic cleansing, and confiscation of honestly earned wealth and…"

Ron, "Honestly earned wealth! Those Jewish 'merchants' were like Marx's capitalists. They continued to accumulate and hoard their money. Meanwhile, the non-Jews in Israel went broke and hungry. It was little more than Jewish genocide."

Bill, "Okay, then why aren't you over in Israel doing your killing thing? Why aren't you fighting the Jews alongside the displaced Arabs? Why aren't you in the Middle East killing a Zionist?"

Ron, "I will someday. Vietnam's the place to be just now. I've got a Jew in my sights, just like Hitler did. I'll get myself a slope head first.

Bill, "For god's sake. Why don't you just buy a pistol from a gun shop in America and walk up to someone wearing a yarmulke on the street and shoot him. You're your own worst enemy."

Ron lapsed into a period of rare silence, "Some advice for you, given only once: Best to define 'enemy' before you call a person one."

Bill held his tongue. Somehow, his assertion of "You're your own worst enemy" had disturbed Ron. Bill sensed he had been warned. He thought, *I'm dealing with a psychopathic pedant.*

Mad or Madness?

What makes a person mad? Not angry, as in riled, but mad, as in insane? What makes a person sociopathic—even pathological, yet seemingly manages to meld into society? Bill had never come across a man like Ron personally, only in text books: a witty and smart person, but one who displayed a bitter humor that discounted any empathy toward another human. Light satire with other people as a façade for a dark soul. Merging easily into the crowd, only to later depopulate part of that crowd.

Frustration

In their uneasy relationship, Ron and Bill had been serving on the same command for a year, sitting on a ship that housed Special Forces and SEALs who conducted raids and assaults on Viet Cong enclaves.

During those times, Bill was reassigned to logistics, and spent much of his time ashore during SEAL/Marine raids and landings. Ron became frustrated with his billet on the ship. He had not been assigned to a unit in the Navy that could kill someone directly. Ron sat passively on the war ship, giving directions to sailors whose cannons lobbed ineffectual shells onto distant Vietnamese landscapes.

They talked past each other about Ron's obsession to kill someone; about Ron's sarcastic remarks about Bill taking an easy way out of life. On and on it went. Overall they were polar opposites, but Bill kept his distance to maintain a relationship between two men who had to share a tiny living space.

Meanwhile, Vietnam was in turmoil and descending into chaos.

One morning, Bill, who had suffered an injury from a beach assault, was recovering in a navy hospital in the Philippines. Half asleep, he was shaken from his slumber by his cabin mate—who was clearly drunk, having snuck into the hospital during a time when most people were having breakfast.

"Bill, I smuggled in some vodka. Here, have a drink with me for us to celebrate," as Ron poured alcohol into an empty coffee cup.

"This had better be a big deal. I'm trying to get some rest. What's going on?"

"I got my orders. As requested, I'm being reassigned to a PT boat."

"You're crazy! That puts you in the Mekong delta. The casualty rate on PT boats in the Delta is out of sight. You'll be an open target."

"Maybe so, but I'm tired of sitting on a ship watching a bunch of jarheads try to shoot up a few gooks. On a PT boat, I can do the shooting myself. I'm going to be second-in-command of the boat. They're outfitted with the latest high caliber machine guns."

"So, you've finally found a way to kill someone."

"Yeah and legally."

"Good luck, you're going to need it."

Ron raised himself from his knees and pocketed his near empty bottle of vodka. As he walked away from Bill's bed, he bade farewell, "Adios, slacker."

After his recovery from the injury, Bill was reassigned to a states-side billet. There, he received a telegram from a former shipmate who informed him that Ron had committed suicide. He killed himself while at a PT boat dock facility on the Mekong Delta. Ron had finally succeeded in his obsession to kill someone: himself.

Bill thought of a quote his dad once read to him, "To take a life is to die a little." Bill thought about this quote. He also thought about Ron: "To take one's own life is to die a lot."

Years later, Bill was visiting the Vietnam War Memorial in Washington, D.C. To this man, it was the most somber and depressing edifice in the nation's capital. As he was viewing Ron's inscription on the black wall, a man and his family stood next to him viewing the same section.

They exchanged short commiserations with each other about the names of interest on the wall. The stranger said his brother died from a misplaced American land mine. He asked Bill what caused the death of his person of interest. Bill's answer: "Enemy fire."

CHAPTER 19

BLIND MAN'S BLUFF

They had placed themselves in the shallow end of the swimming pool. With the liquid to their shoulders, they were bobbing up and down, enjoying the warmth of a summer sun, the coolness of the water and each other's company.

After a while, they made their way to the steps at the end of the pool. Taking canes from the steps banister, they tapped their way to their lounge chairs. There, they toweled off while they kept up their banter.

Weather permitting, each day they came to the pool. They made their way into the water, bobbed up and down for while, and returned to their lounges on the cement deck at the end of the pool.

A young man swam to the pool's end, "Hello, I'm Hal. I'm a condo neighbor. I've been watching you enjoying the water."

"Hello. This is my wife, Molly. I'm James."

"Just wondering, do you two swim?"

James, "Good god, no! I'm scared of ducking my head in the water. I have trouble in the bath tub."

"That's James. I love dipping under water, as long as I can stand on the bottom of the pool. But I don't do much. James is afraid I'll somehow disappear. Imagine, at a public pool, no less."

"How can I know if anyone would help us?"

"James, we're surrounded by our neighbors. Goodness, my love! If I did lose my balance and start to drown, I'm sure they'd pull me from the pool drain."

"Very funny. We should stick to bobbing."

Hal, "One of the reasons I swam by to say hello is I used to be a swimming instructor. I come out here almost every day and do little else but leave with a sunburn. I was wondering if you might like to learn to swim? I need to brush up on my instruction methods. You could be my guinea pigs. In turn, I'd give you free lessons."

"Oh, James, what an opportunity. Let's say yes!"

"I'm not so sure. You know I'm not too good in water."

"Please, let's try it, James, for me"

James' love for his mate overcame his reluctant nature. His somewhat hidden fortitude masked his fear, so he and his wife began the swimming lessons with Hal. But it was slow going for the husband. He was not by nature as adventuresome as his wife. He was usually fearful of taking on a new endeavor. If not fearful, then reluctant. Since he could remember, an unfamiliar place or event created a sense of dread, a fear of the unknown.

Molly kept him from being reclusive. They snow skied, they bowled, they shot darts, all because his wife let him know, "It's time to get up and about." Still, water was particularly dreadful to him.

When Hal introduced a new exercise, it presented a new challenge for James. He sometimes masked his anxiety with sarcasm, "Another blind man's bluff, Hal?" Other times, he remained silent.

Hal understood James' fear. Recently, he had gone through some problems with swimming, so he was not bothered by James' hesitancy and an occasional mocking comment.

No reticence on Molly's part, she took to the water naturally. Hal dubbed her the resident pollywog. But as a team, the rapid gains Molly made were counter balanced by the misgivings of James. As the summer unfolded, their asymmetrical progress became evident.

Still, Molly pushed her reluctant warrior forward. She had entered a new world of pleasure and adventure, and wanted her husband to come along with her. James was resolute in his determination to keep up with Molly and his fear of the water had begun to diminish...somewhat.

Hal offered encouragement to his students as the summer progressed, "I'm proud of you two. You're now bobbing up and down underneath the water. You've learned to blow bubbles. You've opened your eyes underwater and fetched a half-dollar from the floor."

Molly joked, "Yeah, our opening our blind eyes really helped find that half-dollar!"

"Sorry, Molly, force of habit from a swimming instructor. Anyway, you're doing floats on your backs and stomachs, and bringing your feet back down to the pool floor—all by your selves. The back float is one of the biggest hurdles in overcoming what I call aqueous anxiety. Both of you are hurdling those anxieties like Esther Williams. Eh, Johnny Weismuller for James."

The Wiesmuller member of the family thought, *Praise for Ms. Pollywog, not me. Will Labor Day ever come around?*

"Our next step will be to move yourselves through the water while floating on your stomachs. It will be our first exercise demonstrating why people love to swim: propelling their bodies through the water, something like flying, but still on the earth. It's a wonderful sensation."

James, "Here comes another blind man's bluff."

Hal, "Tell me, James, do you enjoy the feeling of the water moving around your body when you're bobbing?"

"It can be pleasant. But I'm not moving, so what's your point?"

Molly, "James, stop it! Stop your contrariness, or I'm leaving this lesson."

James was startled at Molly's outburst, especially one of chastisement. She was low key, and had raised her voice so seldom, he could not recall the last time he had heard his wife—well, snarl. Silently, James nodded his head in acquiescence.

He responded, "Fine. Hal, how do we go about this moving?"

For those of us who can see, we know intuitively how to execute bobbing, as well as floating, gliding, and picking up coins from the floor of the pool. As spectators to these actions, we might not be able to execute them, but we can see how they are done. What is intuitively obvious to those who have sight is far from obvious to those who do not.

Hal, "We gain motion by using one foot to push ourselves away from the side of the pool and go into a float. Just like the stomach float you've been doing. And now, the placing your hands in front of you, which we've been practicing, will act as the bow for your body to move through the water.

"Okay, stand by me at the side of the pool. James to my right, Molly to my left. I'm going to ask both of you to grab my waist and hold me up so I can place my foot on the side of the pool. "

"I'm confused. Why not keep the other foot on the floor, like this one?" as Molly reached her leg around to tap Hal's other leg. She tapped no leg. Where the leg should have been, there was only water."

"You're missing your left leg!"

"Yep, and I've only one hand. Here, James, take my left wrist."

James reached over to grasp Hal's wrist. True to Hal's claim, James found no hand, only a smooth nub.

James, "Can you tell us what happened?"

"I was caught in an explosion while serving as a frogman in Vietnam. I swam with an Underwater Demolition Team. We were conducting a beach survey in an area that intelligence told us was free of the enemy, not even a village nearby. There were four of us, organized as two dual-man squads to look out for each other.

"Our support pickup boat stayed out of sight, just in case a Charlie patrol was walking around the beach. The boat was due to come in at an allotted time to pick us up. We had to swim near the surface, but we were careful to stay hidden from beach recon, part of our training.

"It turned out the intelligence on the area was dead wrong, which resulted in three dead frogmen. A Viet Cong patrol boat caught us off guard. My mates were swimming just below the surface. My partner was swimming close to the other two frogmen. I could see the three of them above me. I was measuring current flows and working several feet under water, a few yards away from their activities.

"The patrol boat probably sighted only three swimmers. Their rifle fire missed us, but they were also using water explosives, a kind of grenade. They tossed them in the water and some exploded next to my mates. One detonated a few feet from me. I never saw it coming, as I was underwater."

"How did you make it back to the boat?"

"I don't remember much after the explosion. I was lucky. The Viet Cong made lousy ordnance, so the impact was not a killer. But it was a stunner. I was knocked dizzy, and my buddies on the near-surface were easy targets. I got farther down into the water and headed for the rendezvous point. Again, I'm not sure what happened during those minutes, but I am certain the habits drilled into me saved my life. I reacted without thinking."

James, "Habits die hard. In your case, they didn't die; probably saved you."

"The habits of training kept me going. Funny, not much different from the habits you and Molly are picking up at this pool. I did things automatically, just like you're doing with a stomach float.

"Anyway, I hoped the pickup boat had heard or saw the attack, but no luck. They were idling too far away, plus underwater explosions don't make much noise. The wind was coming inland, so they never heard the gun fire either. Bad luck again. I eventually made it farther out to sea and put up a flare."

James. "You swam from the attack with only one leg and an arm?"

"Actually one leg and one and a half arms. The leg was useless, more of a drag than anything else. But here I am. The flare brought the pickup boat, and that was it. The Viet Cong boat was milling around the water where my mates had died, and it initially started toward me. I thought I was a goner, but it turned back and left the area.

"I'm sure they knew there was a sub, PT boat, or a destroyer backing up the pickup boat, which was our routine. We radioed in for an aerial attack, but the carrier was too far away for planes to catch the patrol boat. But they did fly in and made sure Charlie did not retrieve my mates.

"Shortly, I was on the destroyer, unconscious. Later, I was told the ship came a-hurrying to the beach. Other frogmen debarked and brought back the bodies of my team members."

Molly, "Did you have any say-so about the operations on your leg and arm?"

"The surgeons had no choice, and I was almost dead anyway. The Subic Bay naval hospital gained two more souvenirs: a leg and a hand."

James, "Were you scared?"

"At that time, no. Didn't enter my mind, but I almost drowned. I think I blacked out once or twice. I remember shedding some ballast, and I was lucky my tanks weren't hit. There's an old saying that has stuck with me from my school days, "The habit of doing one's duty drives out fear."[3] I think my habits got me far enough away from the shore to fire the flare."

James, "Why didn't you tell us about your condition?"

Molly, "Come to think of it, we've not been around you unless you've in the water. You fooled us."

"You didn't tell me you were blind. Why should I tell you I'm missing a couple of body parts?"

James, "Our blindness is obvious. We can't see yours."

" 'Yours' what James? I don't want pity. Do you? If I can swim with one arm and one leg, why can't you swim with two arms and two legs?

"Because you have two eyes and I have none."

"You don't swim with your eyes. You swim with your arms and legs. You're two up on me. I'm more handicapped than you."

---

[3] Attributed to Charles Baudelaire. See *Intimate Journals*, 116.

"Hal, Molly once had sight. I never did. She has a different perspective on this swimming thing. She's seen it, she understands it. I haven't. I don't."

"James, we've done things together. We've learned to ski, to bowl, to throw darts. This is no different."

"It is different, Molly! I nearly drowned when I was a child. I fell off a dock near our home. I couldn't swim, and I was by myself. I don't know how I did it, but I found a dock piling. It was covered with moss, and I kept slipping off. I shouted for god knows how long. Finally, a neighbor came by and fished me out. It shook me, Molly. I still have nightmares of not being able to get out of the water, of slipping away from the piling. "

Molly, "Yes, I wake up from your tossing about, but you've never told me about them until now. ...Gentlemen, it seems our swimming lesson today has become a confessional. I am sorry to disappoint you two, I have nothing to confess, but my husband should be taken behind the wood shed. Why have you not told me about this, James?"

"I'm embarrassed to admit it, but I dread this place. I'm here because you're a fish in water and loving it. Anyway, it's out in the open. The truth is, if you were not having so much fun, I'd be sorry Hal came along. I was doing okay with the bobbing."

Hal, "James, I'm leery of the water, too. I don't have much control, and I can't force myself to do ocean swimming, too much current and tide, too many bad memories. But I've been practicing to swim with my handicap. For me, it's a matter of repetition to overcome my fear. You're no longer afraid of stomach floating, right?"

"No, I'm comfortable."

"Then, let's start the glide work. It's just a small addition to the tummy float."

Thus, James began another quest to overcome his fear: facing it. James was again the reluctant warrior. Game, but reluctant. Molly encouraged him to push away from the sanctity of the side of the pool to glide a few feet. In spite of hesitations, matrimonial rivalry can produce wonders between mates.

"No blind man's bluff, Hal?"

"No blind man's bluff, James. I'm just a few feet away."

The closing summer days saw Molly swimming across the pool. James' advances were more modest, but he managed a few strokes, swimming almost half-way to the other side. But unless Hal was next to him, he stayed at the shallow end. In contrast, Molly was becoming an accomplished swimmer, at ease in the deep water.

The pool was closing on Labor Day, one last day for a one-handed/one-legged swimmer to teach two blind people to swim. In a manner of speaking, the blind was leading the blind. Nonetheless, Hal had succeeded in teaching James and Molly how to execute an American Crawl, as well as a fall over dive: Fall over in the sense that they kneeled down close to the water from the poolside, and with their hands over their heads, fell headfirst into the pool.

Today would be a final challenge for Molly and James, a plunge from the diving board, a narrow, undulating platform about two feet above the water in the pool. For the initiation into this new world, Hal walked each of them to the end of the board. Next, he swam with each one to the end of the board, where he had them reach up and grab hold of the board to gain a sense of its distance from the water.

As always, Molly led the way. And as before, matrimonial pride overrode fear, at least to persuade James to walk the plank. There he stood…frozen. He knew he was the current spectacle at the pool. He and Molly had become poolside celebrities.

James was no longer with Hal on the board. Hal was in the water waiting to assist James to the side of the pool after his dive. James stood alone, moving up and down ever so slightly. The board's motion came more from his tremors than his weight. Molly was standing on the deck, with a mental image of her husband holding his hands, shivering and wavering. In a split second, he could turn around and end his summer of dread.

"Why don't you just have me dive off into the Grand Canyon, Hal?"

"Too far to the water, James. Besides, the Canyon's too big a bluff, even for a blind man."

"Very funny, you've been around Molly too long."

" Come on in, James. Molly did it. It's your last water task for the summer. Just think, you can bask in glory through the winter."

"Blind man's bluff, Hal? Is there water for me to dive into? You didn't have the pool drained on me did you?"

"Give it a go and see for yourself."

"Well, we've come this far."

"Not we, James. Not I. Not Molly. You."

James hesitated for a moment. He then bent over, executed a perfect belly flop, and swam unassisted to the side of the pool.

CHAPTER 20

TOOK SICK

*D*uring the Vietnam War, the idea was to go into sick bay feeling sick and come out feeling well. If not well, then on the road to recovery. The U.S. naval warship—a vessel housing intelligence personnel—was staffed with a doctor and four enlisted medics to take care of the crew, to keep them ship shape.

Each morning after chow, the ship's PA system announced sick call, a signal for under the weather sailors and malingerers to report for treatment. If a sailor or officer showed signs of a malady, he had "took sick," a code—shorthand slang—used by the doctor and medics to tag an alleged illness as legitimate.

"Where's Smith?"

"He took sick. He's in sick bay. Doc's placed him under observation."

The sick bay queue was longer during the first few days out to sea from a liberty port. Recent boot camp sailors, as well as a few seasoned seamen, had made their presence known in the wrong places on the beach and were paying the price. Picking up on the medical slang they heard at sick bay, an infected sailor—having dropped his pants for further inspection—would opine, "I 'took sick' while ashore," hoping for sympathy and special treatment. They took sick from a case of the crabs.

Sick bay contained three rooms. Next to a tiny dispensary was a cubicle used by the doctor for private consultations. The bay had a larger area with several tiered bunk beds to take care of a possible run on sick bay because of a bug among the crew or from the remote possibility of war casualties.

In the past, the latter possibility had indeed been remote, but not now. Until recently, injuries or death from the enemy was an abstract notion, but no longer. The Viet Cong had infiltrated into what was considered a secure zone adjacent to the South Vietnamese city of Danang, which was next to a large harbor in the South China Sea.

All U.S. Navy ships in this zone were alerted when Viet Cong swimmers blew up parts of a Marine causeway at Red Beach. The Marine guards ashore had seen some of the enemy frogmen, but their sightings were too late. After the explosion, the swimmers responded to the Marines' rifle shots by disappearing underwater.

How could that be? Where did they go, and where did they come from? The area, sea and land, was patrolled and had been locked down for several weeks. How did the swimmers penetrate the shield?

An obvious refuge and possible launching pad for the Vietcong frogmen were the many sampans interspersed among the naval vessels. The Vietnamese men in the boats made their living by catching fish, while their American neighbors made their living trying to catch Charlie. The fishermen in these boats kept their distance from the warships. They went about their work silently, plying their trade away from the military vessels.

The fishermen stayed on board their boats during the night. The intelligence operatives on the naval vessels concluded night time made it easier to place Charlie frogmen into the water to attack a causeway, or of more consequence, the hull of a ship.

The reaction to the causeway attack was a full scale security alert within this modest yet potent fleet of ten warships. South Vietnamese and U.S. naval frogmen went into the water to check all U. S. Navy ships' hulls. And no longer would the fisherman be allowed to fish unfettered. Naval patrol boats paid a call on each fishing boat—a formidable task, given the number of boats to visit.

At each sampan, South Vietnamese frogmen and U.S. naval officers took charge. Fishermen were randomly extracted from their sampans, taken aboard a patrol boat, and conveyed to the intelligence ship for further questioning. This program—moving the suspects to a more convenient location—was designed to flush out the causeway bombers and other enemies.

Most of the naval officers on the patrol boats had no war time duty and little experience handling their newly issued .45 pistols. Or for that matter, the possibility of meeting a person they thought might want to kill them. Recently released from their four-year universities, they had fired one single magazine of bullets during their three months of officer candidate school training.

One shaky novice accidentally shot a fisherman while rummaging through his boat. True to the fortunes of war, or misfortunes, the fisherman took sick. …Took sick in that he died from the shot. The ill aiming Ensign was taken off sampan patrols and assigned to less demanding duties.

Once aboard the ship, the fishermen were admitted to sick bay. They went in well, but usually came out sick. South Vietnam and U.S. intelligence operatives guaranteed this outcome from the fishermen's treatment. The resident doctor and his four medics were consigned to another part of the ship to take care of the crew's coughs. Their former place of practice had its bunk beds filled with baffled and damaged fishermen.

The Red Beach causeway bombers were never caught. One fishing boat was found to house a diving mask; no fins; no scuba gear, just one diving mask. The fisherman on whose boat the mask was discovered was declared an enemy and was sent to sick bay for treatment. As with others, he came out less than well.

The fleet surveillance operation was declared successful, even though no confessions were extracted, no bombs or scuba gear were found among the scores of fishing boats. The result of the capturing of a diving mask and one suspected bomber: mission accomplished.

The sampan fishing fleet near the war vessels dispersed. The fishermen left the area for less dangerous waters. For the locals, fish were replaced with yet more rice. Many of the fishermen who took sick from their stay at sick bay never recovered from their stay at a U.S. Navy warship infirmary.

CHAPTER 21

CORNERING THE MARKET

Fools and geniuses are often confused.
—Spoken by a foolish genius

*I*n my work as a venture capitalist, I have lost track of how many crackpot schemes that have come across my desk. Some of the proposals I turned down could have been concocted by Aladdin in his lamp. But on the other hand, I have discovered what might appear as lunacy sometimes makes innovative people rich. Think of Federal Express as one example or Facebook as another.

I view my occupation as that of a *speculation* capitalist. *Venture* seems too tame, slanted against what might appear as foolish ideas. You can make a lot more money by *speculating* than you can by *venturing*. Of course, you can lose a lot more, too. Consequently, I pay close attention to all proposals, even those from the hair brains.

The other day, I asked the man sitting next to me on the train, "Sorry, I'm not sure I heard what you said. Would you mind repeating?"

I was taking a commuter train from Connecticut to Manhattan. It was a five-day grind each week to reinforce my sterling reputation as a Wall Street derivatives trader of instruments which have absolutely no social value. But it was worth the commute. I made money off others' ignorant trust in America's so called capitalism.

My traveling companion was a stranger but a gregarious one. He was also headed for Wall Street. He was full of gestures and words, both of which he directed my way. I had no objection. My book was tepid in tone and my interest in reading it indifferent.

Perhaps he would tell me the news of the day, a common subject of conversation on commuter trains. I had not bothered to check the papers or TV this morning, so I asked my companion about the morning news.

Ignoring my news update request, he responded, "I'm headed for a meeting with a venture capitalist. My partners and I are going to corner the market on urine. Today's the day we've been waiting for!"

Urine, an excretion no one wants to corner, especially inside one's own body. After all, that's one purpose of a human's urinary apparatus: to piss off the liquid to combat being pissed off in the first place.

Saddled with this man for a commute to New York, I put on my Wall Street face and enquired, "Is your specific urine product part of the futures market?"

"Future? The future is now. It's today. Our plans have been hashed out for months and are ready for implementation. We've been waiting for the right time. We are going to create a human urine market."

"Human urine?"

"Absolutely!"

His enthusiasm was evident. Our exchange of news tidbits could wait, "I don't want to come across as negative, but who is going to sell, much less buy human urine? It's always been a waste element in our lives, and it still is."

"That's the present opinion about urine, but in the near future, it will not be."

He seemed to perceive a trace of skepticism on my part. Perhaps my near silent uttering of "What bullshit," gave me away—even though I was making reference to a different excrement.

His pause was brief, "Let me explain. My partners and I have formed a company called Partners in Piss, Inc. We have shortened it to PIPI, pronounced as PEPE...you know, what with the word piss having an image problem, but 'Mama, I have to pe-pe,' has a homey tone to it...Very marketable.[4]

"Besides, we are not going to sell the urine itself. Who would buy something that most people have too much of to begin with. We are going to buy urine."

I undertook another silent uttering, of which he was aware.

"Hold on, sir, just listen. Our *purchase* of urine will be used to *sell* urine based products."

I held my tongue, but retained my initial impression that I had met yet another outlandish hair brainer. I was somewhat put to rest when he informed me of research that had been conducted on the electrical properties of urine. He said it had been scientifically confirmed that the chemical composition of urine made the liquid an ideal substance to charge batteries, such as those in cell phones. He had at least done some homework.

Besides, these sorts of off the wall ideas are what make venture capitalists filthy rich...or abjectly poor. His peculiar

---

[4] Without getting ahead of the story, PIPI had hired a public relations expert who brought with him a jingle expert. She created award-winning jingles using PIPI and Pee Pee as launch pads for the verses. In effect, her efforts brought piss out of the water closet.

notion aroused my curiosity, "Why is human urine such a good battery charger?"

He launched into a highly technical discussion about the electrical virtues of the liquid, so I will not saddle you with his details. In a nutshell, he told me the technology revolved around urine's inherent low levels of organic carbon and its ideal acidity.[5] He waxed on, "In combination, both make for a powerful source of energy."

In the spirit of the conversation, I joined in, "Something like the old cliché, 'piss and vinegar?'"

"Exactly! Say, that would be a fine motto for our product line. You don't by any chance have a trademark on it do you?" I nodded no.

He continued, "We have patents on urine based fuel cells. I'm hoping the meeting today will start the production and shortly the sales," of what he said would make him and his partners rich beyond imagination.

I come from the skeptical side of a venture capitalist (or speculation capitalist, take your pick). I am skeptical but open minded. Naturally, I asked the man venture capitalist questions. Such as, "How is your company going to find the urine to make the fuel cells? How will you capture and store the urine and get it into the fuel cells? Are the fuel cells already built? Have they been tested? How much urine are you talking about? How do you propose to get urine based fuel cells to the market?"

"We have resolved those issues. Plus, our fuel cells perform better than chemical cells. And listen to this: Here's our ace in the hole. We plan on going after the money that the Warren Buffett foundation is giving away to charity and good causes."

Another madcap synapse had fired in this man's head, so I

---

5 "Pee Power," *The Economist*, August 2, 2014, 60.

responded, "But your product would be commercial. It would be a for profit invention. Furthermore..."

I did not have a chance to finish before the man shouted, "You don't catch on. Piss is *renewable energy*! What could be a better cause than to find a new source of replenishable energy? The earth will never run out of piss! Mr. Buffett's Foundation will be pissing in its pants to give us loads of money for such a worthwhile product."

The commuter car's semi-somnolent passengers immediately stirred themselves from their naps and dreams of exploitive glory. Shouting on a commuter train foretold danger: terrorists coming through the car; a stalking insurance salesman; a stockbroker about to shoot himself and other commuters after a bad day at the office. Emergencies like that.

No matter. I also raised my voice. "Why of course! You will not have to wait for the wind to blow its currents though turbine blades, or for the sunshine to power solar cells. All you have to do is keep people drinking."

"Exactly! The fuel for urine renewable energy is no more expensive to manufacture than sipping a glass of water or soda, wine, beer, anything liquid. A fountain of plenty."

My venture capital mind was getting fired up. My frontal lobes were displaying images of dollar signs. But I needed more information, "You avoided my questions about where and how you get your raw supplies."

"That's another ace in the hole for us. We're going after the easy way to get urine. One of our key marketing points to Wall Street, which is embedded into our presentation so often that it will melt their resistance. Here's one of our mottos: 'The piss passing through urinals is the pathway to profit!'

"We'll let our competitors deal with those inefficient commodes. They mix water with the pee and other offal, which dilutes the electrical conductivity of pure urine.

"Our plan is to pay a small fee to urinal owners for the purchase of the piss passing through their urinals. We've designed a urinal drain that diverts the urine into a storage tank. We even have sensors that check the flow of the urine passing out of the person's body. After all…"

I had to interrupt, "This person would necessarily be a man."

"Of course! How many urinals have you encountered in women's rest rooms?"

If I were a sensitive sort, I might have been offended that he was implying I, a stalwart male, paid calls to the female retreat. But I was merely laying the groundwork for later informing him that his plan automatically reduced his source of urine energy by 50 percent. But he was on a roll and took no further notice of my observation.

He continued, "As I was saying, after the pisser has finished his task, and we've captured his urine, the rinse water is automatically turned on but diverted away from our now closed urine tank.

"Think of it! After all, it will be newly found money for the urinal owners. Even more, for selling us their customers' urine, we'll keep their restrooms spotless, as part of the contract."

I was intrigued, especially with the idea of clean public restrooms, a rarity unto itself. Maybe this peculiar commuter was not so peculiar after all. My caution was ebbing, "It seems to have been thought out."[6]

"Absolutely. We even have a trademark name for our product."

"Oh, not too keen on Piss and Vinegar?"

"Nah, just joking. Besides, vinegar is not part of our

---

6 Ibid.

product, otherwise we would have to call our masterpiece something like Vinegar and Pee. Not much pizzazz in that name, so to speak. "

"Okay, so what is the name of your product?"

"We're giving it a term all Americans adore: 'Piss-Off!' Cool, eh?"

"Yeah, the name will get the public's attention. Captures the American attitude."

As the train left Connecticut and entered New York, I began to realize the man was excited, but not because he often had to use a toilet and pay for its use. He had devised a way to use a toilet and have the toilet pay him.

Nonetheless, my skepticism was still evident, "It seems you will need a lot of urine to fuel the cells. That's why I raised the subject of automatically losing one-half of your sources of urine. There's the 'economy of scale' problem. How much urine do you need to capture in order to power enough fuel cells to make a profit?"

"I should have answered you earlier. Do you know how much urine is produced each year? Of course you don't. It is 6.4 trillion liters.[7] We only need to tap in to a small part of this market. Some changes to a urinal will be needed but not many, modest in comparison to the profits we will make.

"There's even more to our idea. After the installation is complete, we will have maintenance free organic pumps for our use. Consider the low overhead: just a couple of male kidneys and an associated appendage. No oiling of the parts. Even better, no parts replacements. The low overhead practically guarantees our success."

Silence fell from this entrepreneur's lips as we neared our destination. I remained skeptical, but I admit I was coming

---

[7] Ibid.

around. "I'm not one to toss water, or for that matter, urine onto someone's fire. But I must say, I detect a flaw in your scheme." After all, if we capitalists do not ferret out faults in a proposal, we would shortly run out of capital and associated adventures.

"That's what almost everyone has said, and we are going to prove them wrong. Today will be the vindication of our quest."

"Maybe, but how are you going to compete with the shale/gas revolution? Fracking is advanced today, so cost effective that new technologies for energy have taken a back seat. How can something be successful that is associated with what will be an obvious public relations challenge. After all, piss *is* piss, pee *is* pee. In addition to a significant public image problem, Piss-Off! will have to compete with fracking as a cheap energy source."

My commuting companion gave me a surprised look, "You've not heard?"

"Heard what?"

"Last night, West Texas collapsed into a gigantic hole."

"What?"

"Yeah. The fracking extractions led to huge disruptions and earthquakes in the sub-surfaces of the West Texas tectonic plate. Last time I checked this morning, Texas was no longer the second largest state in the Union.

"And here's more. Early this morning, parts of Northeast Montana slid over into North Dakota. You missed some big news. That's why I'm heading into town: to launch Piss-Off! It's now a competitive source of energy to fracking."

Realizing I should have watched the morning news, I decided to venture into speculation. This one was just too good to be true, but it was true, "Does your company need any more venture capital? That's my line of work. My company would be interested. What do you say?"

"Piss-off!"

"I take that as a yes?"

"You sure do. Besides, a bird in hand is worth two in the bush. Shall I accompany you to your office?"

* * *

Given that the fracking doomsayers' warnings came true, Piss-off! proved to be a huge success. The IPO (dubbed as the Initial Piss Offering to move potential investors into the spirit of the event) set new records for gathering capital. True, a massive advertising campaign was needed to convince the public that a cell phone containing piss was harmless to the ear and mouth of the cell phone user. But if a person could be convinced to drink recycled water that was known to be once generously mixed with human urine and other assorted wastes, a closed, encased urine fuel cell was of little concern.

However, the fracking industry did not take earthquakes and sink holes as a defeat. Even though Texas was a diminished landscape from its former topography, even though the Montana/North Dakota merger upset the balance of power in gerrymandered America, the frackers discovered huge shale deposits in the Rocky Mountains. It was a geographical treasure brought about by tectonic shifts and upheavals millions of years ago.

What made this form of mountain fracking even more attractive was the fact that when the fracked area collapsed in a mountain range, it did not create a massive sink hole. With the disappearance of a mountain here and there, the Great Plains of North America became even greater.

This geographical godsend delighted local ranchers. Exercising their rights as members of America's welfare programs, they immediately herded their cattle and sheep to graze on newly found and deeply discounted government top soil.

CHAPTER 22

FLOOR PLAN

*J*eb saw the exchange of cash. He watched the customer count out several one-hundred dollar bills and hand them to the used car lot manager, Frank, who was Jeb's temporary boss. Ordinarily, this transaction would not have caught Jeb's attention. Customers often paid cash for a car purchase, and several vehicles were sold each day. Jeb had paid little attention to Frank's handling of these payments, but something about this transaction caught Jeb's eye. The same customer had bought a car last week. This purchase was his second of the week. Three cars in two weeks?

Jeb was not by nature suspicious, but he was curious. He watched as Frank took the money and shuffled it in his hands as he recounted the cash. Twenty one-hundred dollar bills.

Jeb's stay at the used car lot was to have been one week, a short stint the EZer Loans Company had set up as part of his training. His final job was to be a field collection agent for EZer Loans. If his collection efforts were not successful, he would be responsible for repossessing the wayward customer's car, which would usually end up at the car lot where Jeb was receiving his training.

Jeb was a recent hire at EZer Loans, a firm specializing in quick contract loans to people who could not obtain financing at conventional banks and credit unions. Repossessions were a normal part of loan sharking operations, and EZer Loans's usurious interest rates made up for the expenses of repossessing a car.

EZer Loans made much of its money by bank rolling a car dealer's inventory of vehicles, a practice known in the business as floor planning. The finance company paid the car manufacturer for the cars and put them on the lots of car dealers. The dealer paid the finance company interest on each car, essentially a short term loan. As the cars were sold, the dealer paid back its loan to the finance company.

EZer Loans had another relationship with several used car dealers, those that did not have a loan department. These car dealers steered loans for the used car purchases to EZer Loans. "Have I got a deal for your loan! EZer Loans offers a special rate for our customers. You won't find a better setup than what EZer Loans will offer you. Their motto is: *EZ loans make for easier payments.* Just sign here and we'll get your loan going with EZer Loans."

The car lot where Jeb was receiving his training was unlike EZer Loans's usual car dealer customers. EZer owned this lot, the buildings, and the cars themselves. This part of the company employed Frank, another salesman named Jim, the trainee Jeb, Charlie, the head mechanic, and Charlie's "staff," another mechanic.

Some of the cars had been repossessed by EZer's field collection agents. Others had been purchased from people who were pressed for money and sold their cars cheaply to EZer Loans. The company's goal was to sell the vehicles quickly, turning over the inventory made for an increased income flow. The company was in the loan shark business, but the used car lot operations brought in substantial income.

Part of Jeb's training was learning to hot wire vehicles. Newer models were quite difficult to hot wire. Increasingly, hot wiring was becoming a lost art. EZer Loans and the car dealers had duplicate keys for most of the cars, especially the new models fresh off the car dealer's lot. If a collection agent was hot on the trail of a deadbeat customer, he kept a set of the vehicle's keys with him. He often had to take possession of a vehicle with little advance notice, usually during a successful search for the car's whereabouts. It made no sense to spend precious time going back and forth to the car dealer or to an EZer office to obtain the keys.

Charlie and his one mechanic made repairs and assessed a vehicle's road worthiness. Rarely did Charlie declare a vehicle to be in anything but tip top shape. He would often leave his garage, located on the used car lot, to talk with potential buyers and bolster the salesman's claims about the car's rock solid integrity. He was good at what he did, including his repair work as well as his backing up the salesman's claims.

Jeb was also tasked with additional chores. Each afternoon, he would drive one of the repossessed or recently purchased vehicles to EZer Loans's branch office to deliver sales contracts and pick up company correspondence. Frank would place the papers and money from the sales in an envelope, seal it and send Jeb to Charlie. Charlie would assign Jeb a vehicle for the trip, which allowed it to be test driven. "Jeb, use the green Chevy; it's next to the garage. Just did a tune up. Let me know how it runs."

The lessons with Charlie were the high light of Jeb's days at the used car lot. The remainder of his time was spent listening to Frank and Jim extol the virtues of the vehicles to potential buyers. If Frank and Jim were occupied, Jeb would try out his meager sales skills on a prospective buyer. On one occasion, Jeb actually sold a car, at which time Frank stepped in and closed the deal.

Jeb was scheduled to return to the branch office the following week to begin debt collection training, but Jim was called out of town on family matters. Jeb's boss at the branch office directed Jeb to stay on the lot until Jim returned. Jeb did not mind the extended assignment. He and Charlie had warmed to each other with the mechanic taking the young man under his wing and teaching him the ins and outs of car repair. Charlie was a natural teacher. Patient by nature, he knew his trade well and shared it with his new friend.

It was during this time that Jeb noticed the EZer Loans car lot had several repeat customers. He remembered one man who had bought a four-door sedan the week before. Early in the second week, Frank sold another sedan to him. Later in the week, the same customer bought a used SUV. It was on this occasion that he watched the man hand $2,000 to Frank.

It was not as if Jeb was covertly spying, but he was intrigued and stayed a bit closer to the men during this third purchase. One person buying three cars within a few days fascinated him. He mentioned his observations to Frank.

Frank paused, a pause even Jeb noticed. Frank then responded, "The man flips cars. I give him a good deal. He buys a car from us—say that $2,000 transaction—and sells it for markup above what he pays EZer. My job is to move the inventory. If I don't, the lot gets overrun with repossessions. These car flippers are a godsend.

"We got it going both ways. We collect late fees and accumulated interest from the deadbeat car owner. The owner has to pay us, else we take him to court. It's us or lawyer's fees. We can afford to sell cars on the cheap 'cause we buy them on the cheap or take possession of them on the cheap."

Even with Frank's explanation, Jeb started to ask why EZer Loans would want to sell cars at a low enough price to allow someone to make a living flipping EZer's inventory. But he did not. Shrugging his shoulders, he said to himself, *To each his own.* Still, doubt lingered in Jeb's mind.

The ride from the car lot to the EZer Loans's branch office took a driver over the chaotic freeways of Los Angeles. For the trip the day of the brief conversation with Frank, Jeb took an off ramp to a side street before reaching the office. He pulled over to a curb, stopped the car, turned off the ignition, picked up the sealed envelope and opened it. Thumbing through the contracts he found the paperwork on the used SUV sale. It was signed by seller Frank and the buyer for a price of $1,800, which was also enclosed.

Jeb knew someone was scamming. For certain, at least two of the scammers were Frank and the buyer, but maybe Frank was in league with others. This scam was not much money, but two hundred dollars here and there could add up to a healthy payoff.

Jeb wished he had not been so curious. He could be wrong. After all, he knew little about the used car business. What if he informed his branch manager and nothing was amiss? Maybe Frank had a setup with EZer Loans, even the branch manager. What to do? Go to Charlie, he trusted the man, and Charlie knew the business.

* * *

The next day, when he and Charlie were alone in the garage, Jeb took the opportunity to reveal what he discovered about the scam. After Jeb's story, Charlie remained silent for a while. He sighed, then turned to Jeb.

"What did the branch office say about the opened envelope?"

"Nothing. I stopped at a drug store and bought another one."

"Good thinking. Jeb, it's an old trick of the trade in the used car business. I've seen it more times than I can count. For that $2,000 sale, Frank reported only $1,800 to the branch office. Frank and the buyer will split the $200 difference.

"The used car business is messy—buying and selling prices vary a lot. Whoever keeps the books can fudge 'em. It's illegal, but it's not all that hard to pull off. Looks like you got the goods on him, Jeb."

"Yeah, Charlie, but I saw this man buy three cars within a few days. No telling how many scammers Frank's dealing with. What do I do? I'm over my head. I was tempted to go to the branch manager yesterday after opening that envelope. But I wanted to ask for your advice first. I gotta tell someone, Charlie, else I'm as guilty as Frank. "

"Okay, if you need to spill the beans, then you have no choice. When you make the run to the office today, you should tell the branch manager what you've discovered. And don't say a word to Frank. You might be in danger. Get it off your shoulders, and fast.

"Look, this could be a risky situation for you and now me. But that's all right. You didn't know what to do. For god's sake, Jeb, don't act nervous when Frank gives you the next envelope for the branch office. Take the envelope and come straight to me for a car."

"Will do, Charlie. And thanks. I know I have put you in a ticklish situation."

"You did the right thing. See you shortly."

* * *

Jeb, "I've got the envelope, Charlie."

Charlie, "Good, now get out of here. Take the black Ford that's behind the garage. I've been doing some work on it. Let me know how she feels."

* * *

Police officer, "The papers in the glove compartment show this address. Is that correct?"

Frank, "Yes, officer, those papers are for a car owned by EZer Loans. It's part of our inventory at this lot. My assistant is using the car for a run to the branch office. What's the problem?"

Officer, "I'm sorry to inform you that your assistant is dead. It appears he lost control of the car and crashed on the Harbor Freeway. It was a mess. From what we can tell at this point, the car rammed a car in front of it, then was hit by several trailing cars. It appears the accelerator pedal was the cause of the accident. The first check of the car showed the pedal was stuck to the floor, but we can't say for certain. The investigation's just started. At this point, we want to speak with the person responsible for the maintenance of that car."

Frank, "That's Charlie. He's the best. Follow me, he's next door in the garage."

* * *

Frank, "Charlie, these officers want to know about that Ford—the black one—we got in last week."

Charlie, "What about it?"

Frank, "Jeb had a wreck on the Freeway. The car was totaled. Looks like the accelerator pedal stuck to the floor. Jeb is dead."

Charlie paused, "Jeb crashed the black Ford? That can't be. I'm working on two Fords, both of them behind the garage. But I told him to take the blue Ford.

Officer, "Well, something went wrong. Let's take a look at the other Ford," as the men walked around to the back of Charlie's garage.

Charlie, "I'll be damned! Here's the blue Ford. Jeb got in the wrong car. Blue Ford, black Ford, he musta' heard me wrong."

CHAPTER 23

CRYPTO SUICIDE

"Mr. Rawlings, the admiral wants to see you in his quarters." Ensign Rawlings was surprised by this statement. Junior officers were rarely called on to visit the admiral's office. Their superiors, the senior officers, performed this task. Something unusual was up.

After this terse announcement, the seaman promptly left the Ensign's cabin. This small enclave was located in officer's country aboard a U.S. Navy warship operating in the South China Sea. Officer's country was to be transited quickly by enlisted men, and only in the pursuit of their duties. Casual short cuts through this part of the ship by non-officer personnel were not permitted.

The time was 0600 (6 am). Ensign Hal Rawlings had been up all night in the ship's communications facility, nicknamed the "shack." He was tired but did not lie down. He paused a few seconds in his stateroom to splash his face with cold water.

Aside from the periodic work in the communications

shack, his normal duty was in the cryptography room where he assisted the lead crypto officer, LTJG Mac Sharp. Their responsibility was to keep this highly secret area of the ship operating properly. With selected senior enlisted men, and a few other officers, they encrypted and decrypted top secret messages. However, only a few officers were cleared to decrypt *flash* messages, so identified in the unencrypted header of a message.

To heighten Rawlings' fatigue, the evening and early morning hours had been frantic. An unusual number of encrypted messages had come in from the communications center in Hawaii. But the man took a fait accompli attitude toward his work. No one asked him to join the Navy, and he loved cryptography.

Besides, he was at sea most of the time, which provided a window of opportunity for his wife to complete her graduate work in San Diego before they started a family. Rawlings could not understand why naval officers brought their families halfway around the world. They lodged themselves in uninviting Philippine hotels while their husbands sailed away from them.

The wives often ended up feeling abandoned and alone. Neither officer nor wife grasped the difficulty of such a situation when they were planning this adventure from their secure stateside home. Ensign Rawlings and his wife were practical people. They decided for the wife to remain in the States.

Emergency Sortie

For this story, we shall learn the communications flagship and accompanying vessels were ordered to sail from Subic Bay, Philippines, to a selected location off the coast of Vietnam.

A top secret message from the Commander in Chief, Pacific (CINCPAC) in Hawaii ordered them to get underway as soon as possible. The time of 0800 (8 am) the next day was set for sailing.

Several cargo and personnel vessels were to follow as soon as they could be loaded with Marines and supplies. These operations would not take long. Like the ship in which Ensign Rawlings was billeted, the other vessels and their contents, inert or organic, stayed in a near-ready mode for sailing.

South Vietnam's government was in danger of collapsing. Nearby Indonesia was nearing chaos. Both countries posed potential dangers to American citizens who lived in those countries.

Uncle Sam's navy was responsible for taking aboard U.S. citizens who might be in danger, especially military personnel and civil servants mandated to serve in foreign places. But Uncle's safety net also protected other U.S. citizens who had voluntarily deposited themselves onto foreign soil, some to gather souls for God's flocks, some to gather dollars for themselves. All were protected by the United States government.

Destroyer escorts would also sortie to protect the task force against enemy ships. Of course, America's current enemies in the South China Sea, the Viet Cong of south Vietnam and the Vietminh of north Vietnam, had no navies to speak of, much less submarines. The Chinese Communists had a few run down pre-WWII vessels. They were not foolish enough to take on America's armada. Nor was the Soviet Union, whose strategy was to provide money and supplies to its Cold War ally, North Vietnam.

But a military command must be prepared. One never knew if a *Lusitania* incident might be lurking over the horizon. Thus, a destroyer escort for the vessel on which Mr. Rawlings resided was ordered up by CINCPAC.

The fleet was to make for the coastline near Saigon. Rawlings' ship was to sail first and act as a communications relay point for other ships headed for Vietnam that did not have sophisticated communications equipment. Some of the older destroyers had only Morse code machines. Rawlings' Boy Scout days of learning Morse code for his First Class ranking had impressed the radiomen who reported to him.

During one at sea exercise, Rawlings keyed in the news to nearby ships that Cassius Clay (later Muhammad Ali) had defeated Sonny Liston. One notable response came from a salty chief radioman on a nearby destroyer, "Son, you could use some more practice." The chief did not realize he was admonishing an officer. Although it did not matter, the story became a running joke among the amphibious task force ships in the Western Pacific: *An officer knowing the Morse code, actually doing something. How unique!*

Around 2030 (8:30 pm) the previous evening, Rawlings was interrupted during the showing of a movie in the officers' wardroom. Master Chief Radioman Jameson—the highest ranking enlisted man in the Communications Department—quietly entered the wardroom.

Locating his boss, he nearly whispered to the seated officer, "Mr. Rawlings, a top secret, *flash* message just came in from CINCPAC. Mr. Sharp has the 2000-2400 watch (8 pm – midnight) and can't do a decryption just now; too much incoming traffic for him to review and mark up for distribution.

"Sir, something's going on. The other officers cleared for crypto are ashore. Mr. Sharp told me to request your immediate presence at the shack and crypto room."

"Very well, Chief. I'll go down to the shack, check in with Mr. Sharp, and do the decryption."

"Aye, sir," as the chief made a hasty exit, followed almost as quickly by Ensign Rawlings. The chief was authorized to perform most of the decryptions, but not a flash message. Rawlings was usually summoned to the crypto room to decipher flash messages. He was the best of the decryption personnel aboard the ship.

Rawlings left the movie and headed for the comm shack. He entered the area, which was hardly a shack. The word *shack* was a slang term from the old days when U.S. Navy ships set aside a small nook to store a ship-to-shore/ship-to-ship radio setup and sometimes a Morse code telegraph. The radio shack on this ship contained rooms housing tons of telecommunications gear, far beyond primitive telegraphs. The locked crypto room was an even more secure area located at the rear of the comm shack.

The communications gear on this ship was the best and latest the U.S. Navy had to offer. It cost the taxpayer millions of dollars. After all, it was the flagship for a two star admiral and his staff, a command that was responsible for naval and marine amphibious operations in the Western Pacific.

The admiral, his chief-of-staff and his 100 man compliment of U. S. Navy, Marine officers, and enlisted men rode this ship as "guests" of the ship's officers and crew, whose job was to support this staff. They were guests in the sense that the admiral was the immediate superior of the skipper of the ship whose sole function was to support the admiral's staff. It could be a delicate political arrangement, but one that had worked well enough during exercises, wars, and skirmishes around the world for over thirty years.

As he entered the shack, Hal Rawlings greeted Mac Sharp, "Hey, Mac, are you headed ashore after your watch?"

Mac, "My first priority! The kids will be in bed, and my honey and I will have some privacy for a change. Too bad you don't have your wife with you, Hal. You could be living in tropical paradise on the base. Maid service for a quarter an hour. If you want, cooks for the same. Lawn boys, for a dollar a day. We haven't made a bed or mowed a lawn since leaving San Diego."

Hal, "Yeah, I know. My stateroom's like a hot skillet, and I'm sharing it with three other stinking Ensigns. But I'm not concerned. Hell, Mac, you and I are at sea most of the time anyway, and my wife's only two semesters from getting her masters. She's doing fine, so am I. Tall cotton takes time to grow, Mac."

Mac, "I married to be with my family, Hal, not float around doing nothing."

Hal, "Then you chose the wrong branch of the service. Probably should have joined the air force. You're getting no sympathy from me, my friend. By the way, I better start setting those crypto rotors. The admiral will see the time stamp indicating when CINCPAC's message arrived at our ship."

Mac, "Yeah, here it is, and I've got news. While the chief was looking for you, another flash crypto message came in. Here the other is. Something is going on."

Hal, "Something *is* up, Mac. OK, I'll get them decoded and let you know what's happening."

Mac, "Don't forget to tell the admiral."

Hal, "Very funny. That's the only reason we're aboard this ship, to deliver high profile messages to his excellency."

Mac, "Well, I mentioned it because I've already overlooked one of the emergency standby procedures."

"Yeah?"

Mac, "After receiving the flash message, I notified the ship's OOD [officer of the deck] to pipe the admiral and chief-of-staff drivers to the quarterdeck and remain on standby. They need to get these messages to the senior officers' quarters ashore as fast as possible."

Hal, "Yeah, flashes are hot potatoes. So?"

Sharp, "But I forgot to tell the OOD to have the motor pool get their cars to the pier."

Rawlings, "Mac, the drivers and the motor pool know one goes with the other! And the OOD takes care of those details.

"Mac, are you a bit wound-up? Take it easy. Look, it's all part of the driver pipe-down procedure. And you should know that fact, boss man. What'd you have for dinner anyway? Here…listen."

Rawlings turned on the OOD-quarterdeck intercom: "OOD, comm shack here, over."

"Go ahead. Over."

Rawlings, "Jim, are the admiral and chief-of-staff drivers and their vehicles in standby? Over."

"Aye, ready and waiting. Over."

"Very well. Two couriers will be coming to the quarterdeck shortly with pouches for the admiral and chief-of-staff, and messages for your information and for the skipper. Over."

"Roger. Out."

Hal, "There you are, Mac, take a deep breath. This is not exactly Pearl Harbor."

Mac, "Yeah, thanks. I tend to overreact…guess it's part of the family tree. We jump at our shadows sometimes. I swear, there's times when I feel my brain has shut down on me."

Hal, "Now's the time you tell me this? Buck it up, boss. We've only got a small window to get things done."

A Crypto Babe Ruth

During the early years of the Vietnam "conflict," the U.S. Navy was still using WWII cryptographic equipment. The process of encryption and decryption with this system was a tedious process. The operation entailed manipulating several metal rotors to specific positions identified by letters of the alphabet. Their positions were based on a private encryption/ decryption key. The sender and receiver had to use the same key if the encryption and decryption operations could take place correctly.

The rotors were placed into an instrument resembling a typewriter. The machine encrypted clear text into code that was nonsense to anyone reading its output. Of course, a receiving machine that had set its rotors based on the private key values could render the code into the original clear text.

While attending cryptographic training in San Diego, Hal Rawlings sometimes rotated one of the wheels to an incorrect position. Because he was encrypting a message erroneously, he soon earned the joking derision of the other men in the room who were tasked with setting their machines to the correct code and reading his message. At the receiving end, when he was the decoding operator, he sometimes again set the rotors to incorrect positions, which resulted in yet more cipher text, unintelligible to anyone else but the sender of the message.

During those training days, Rawlings stayed after hours, building his muscle memory to move the cylinder positions to the correct places, to the correct letters. After a while, he was able to set the rotors quickly. When he reported to Amphibious Forces Seventh Fleet in the Western Pacific, he was a crypto Babe Ruth. Whenever flash messages were to be coded or decoded, everyone went looking for Rawlings.

Back to the Emergency Sortie

Within a few moments, Rawlings emerged from the crypto room. "Mac, we've gotta' get moving. CINCPAC is moving our task force out of port ASAP."

Mac, "Whoa! Where to?"

Hal, "Out of Subic and toward Vietnam. Some shit's coming down. Suggest you initiate the emergency sortie protocol."

Mac did not respond immediately…"So much for a visit with my honey and kids. Say, doesn't the emergency sortie order start with the OOD informing the skipper?"

Hal, "You know that already! What the hell's come over you? The OOD must inform the ship's captain about such a CINCPAC message, and the captain must direct the OOD to alert the crew and deliver messages to the staff's admiral and the chief-of-staff at their on-base quarters.

"Then tell me, boss man, how can the OOD initiate this protocol if he doesn't know about the emergency in the first place? For a crypto alert, it must start with the comm watch officer in the comm. shack. That's you!

"I'll get us started," as Hal flipped a switch on the watch officer's desk console to reach the OOD. "Comm shack to OOD, over."

"OOD, over."

"Jim, this is no drill. Initiate task force emergency sortie protocols. Repeat: initiate task force emergency sortie protocols. Seaman Jordon is on his way to the quarterdeck with the CINCPAC sortie order. Deliver ASAP to the skipper and his executive officer. Over."

"Roger, I'll send alerts to the protocol list for this procedure. Out."

Controlled bedlam followed shortly. Within minutes, every hand on the ship was executing his part of the emergency sortie plan. Procedures were initiated to pass information to the staff and ship's crew hierarchy, which would cascade down in a short time to (almost) all hands who could be found in the wildest Navy port in the Western Pacific, Olongapo.

Rawlings, "Mac, look. The second message that came in is for you, the staff crypto officer. CINCPAC wants our staff to establish a separate crypto channel between Hawaii and our command."

Mac, "You're kidding!"

"Nope, we'll use different crypto keys from those used by other Seventh Fleet ships that have crypto gear. It looks like CINCPAC wants a channel only to our amphibious staff. So, let's get moving."

… "Mac, are you OK? You're not doing anything. This last message is a *personal* note from CINCPAC to our crypto department. You should feel honored! Ha."

Mac, "I feel singled-out. Jezz. Our department has direct access to CINCPAC. Big responsibility on us crypto officers. Something is going on over there that might need the Marines. I'll bet the brass doesn't want any scuttlebutt leaking about the situation."

Hal, "Other staff officers are on the distribution list for receipt of a copy of the message. We just need to get the messages to the admiral and his chief-of-staff. And that's why they call us the amphibious navy. We go anywhere. Anyway, I'll bet this alert is not coming from Hawaii directly. It's coming from Washington, and channeled through Hawaii."

Mac, "Washington! Damn, we've got a situation here."

Hal, "Don't sweat it, Mac. A separate crypto channel from CINCPAC to our staff's admiral? That's a piece of cake. We use a separate machine with rotors set up for the reserved codes. It's no big deal. We can keep both channels going but use the same radio frequency for the two different encrypted messages. We never have to go through the fleet to alter frequencies for this traffic. If anyone other than CINCPAC receives the new encryptions, it's just garbage."

Mac, "But that will take a separate set of keys beyond our routine rotations, and we don't have them aboard. They're controlled by the COMSEC (Communications Security) units that are based ashore and given only to authorized commands. The COMSEC unit here in Subic keeps the keys. We can't do anything."

Hal, "That's the entire point of the second message! Look, it's copied to all the COMSEC units in the Western Pacific. All we need to do is drive over to the local COMSEC shack and pick up these special sets of crypto keys.

"Look, Mac, for the next few minutes, only the two of us and a handful of men on this ship and base are aware of what has just happened. We can stand here and debate logistics all night. We've got the sortie protocols started, and we know things will take over by themselves.

"One of the boilers is always in standby. Most of the ship's crew is on board. We're close to being on our way.

"Mac, listen up. Just have a driver take a jeep and you to the COMSEC shack before we sail and bring back those separate sets of keys. I'll call the OOD to get a jeep ready on the dock. Get moving!"

Mac, "But I can't check out those keys by myself, Hal. You know that two officers or an officer and chief petty officer have to sign the receipt for the material at COMSEC."

Hal, "Mac, listen up again! For now, this ship has only two officers aboard who are crypto cleared for flash messages: you and me. We both can't leave the ship under these conditions. We need a crypto officer aboard, and I'm faster at the rotors than you, and COMSEC is copied on both messages anyway.

"The message states the other crypto channel must be activated by 0800. We've got plenty of time to activate but not much time to get the keys. Just get them stowed in the crypto bag, bring them back, and I'll inventory them with you after you return. Let's meet in the crypto room at 0615.

"I'm assuming the con for the watch *and* the crypto room. Take Chief Jameson to COMSEC. He's authorized to be the second signer for the material.

"Don't get creepy on me, Mac. Take a deep breath, get yourself and the Chief into the jeep, and bring back those keys. It's a simple job, just need to do a little bit of improvising."

Mac, "Right, but I still have to use those moth-eaten WWII crypto bags. Hal, they've got tears in them! The fasteners don't even work. I caught you dropping a crypto package from one of those bags last week, and you won't be around to back me up at COMSEC. Why don't we use the new bags that came in last month?"

Hal, "Those new bags have not been reinforced with extra canvas and thread. Can you believe it? A piece of canvas has not been cleared for top secret. Weird Navy stuff: Bos'n locker is too busy making new decorative riggings for the admiral's railings and chief-of-staff's ladders. What a waste.

"And you are beginning to piss me off, boss. I respectively request you get Chief Jameson out of his bunk and the two of you get moving."

"Okay," as LTJG Sharp leaves the shack.

Crypto Confusion

Mr. Rawlings, the Admiral wants to see in you in his quarters. This thought resonated in Rawlings' mind as he made his way to senior officers' country, He asked himself: *Why would the Commander of Amphibious Forces Seventh Fleet want to see a lowly junior crypto officer? Besides, I need to return to the crypto room to get the special keys placed in the inventory. I'll roust Mac, and we'll get the second crypto machine set up. ...Oh well, plenty of time. Mac's probably catching some shuteye after a long night... maybe he went home to bid farewell to his wife. The material is in locked bags in the crypto room. We've got enough time to set the ciphers on the other machine. The admiral knows we'll have a private channel to CINCPAC by 0800. No big deal.*

Upon entering the admiral's expansive cabin, the junior officer beheld the admiral, his chief-of-staff, his personal aide, the head of the communications department (Commander Jensen), the staff legal officer, intelligence department heads for the admiral's staff, and two Marine officers of unknown identity.

Admiral, "Mr. Rawlings, when and where did you last see Mr. Sharp?"

Rawlings, "Sir, around 2345 [11:45 pm] last night in the comm shack. He and Chief Jameson drove to COMSEC, got back to the ship, and stowed the material in the crypto room.

"I stayed on comm watch most of the night, due to the other crypto officers being away from the ship. Mr. Sharp and Chief Jameson were beat. I assume Mr. Sharp headed for his base housing to get in a couple hours with his wife. The Chief headed for his bunk for a few hours sleep.

"Mr. Sharp and I agreed to be back at the crypto room at 0615…just a few minutes from now…do the inventory, and set up the other machine after breakfast."

Commander Jensen joins the conversation, "Mr. Rawlings, Mr. Sharp is missing. He hasn't shown up at his base housing. His wife called the OOD to ask him to find her husband and have him call her. He can't be found on the ship. The local shore patrol was alerted…no luck."

Rawlings, "Sirs, Mr. Sharp would not break a rule as serious as not staying on this ship or at his housing during an alarm condition. I work under him. He's a stickler for protocol and procedure. Any violation of rules bothers him.

"I do recall the emergency sortie and the CINCPAC notice about the special crypto keys did rattle him a bit. He seemed to take the message about the second crypto channels as a personal note from CINCPAC to him. But he and the Chief made the run to COMSEC just fine."

Chief-of-Staff, "Given the urgency stated in the CINCPAC messages, the comm department got caught with its pants down," as the chief-of-staff glared at Commander Jensen.

"Given the situation, Mr. Sharp made a good decision on keeping at least one crypto-flash officer onboard the ship and having Chief Jameson accompany Mr. Sharp to COMSEC. But why didn't you go, Mr. Rawlings? You're the junior officer."

Commander Jensen interjected, "Captain, Mr. Rawlings was the right choice. He's the best and most accurate crypto operator on the ship. A mis-set rotor can waste precious minutes."

Admiral, "Then we can only confirm our suspicions that Sharp went AWOL or tossed himself overboard. We've alerted coast guard units to look for him, but we must clear the task force from this bay. We can't delay our rendezvous deadline off Saigon."

Hal had been waiting his turn, "Committed suicide! With all respect gentlemen, how can we possibly know this? My hunch is that he's on foot somewhere on the base headed for his family. He wasn't thinking clearly last night."

Admiral, "Mr. Rawlings, I wanted to learn more about the last time you saw Mr. Sharp before we let you know about this situation. One of the crypto officers who had returned from liberty found this note in the crypto room early this morning. That's why you're here."

Hal, I mucked this one up big time. I lost a set of keys when returning to the ship last night. I started the inventory before you showed up at the crypto room and discovered one of the special channel key sets was missing. I bear the ultimate responsibility, as I was senior officer for this task. Don't blame Chief Jameson.

As they say, 'you go to war with what you've got.' We just had some shitty gear. But we both had reservations about those dilapidated crypto bags. I wish now I had used the new bags that came in last week, even without the canvas reinforcements.

Most of all, I bear responsibility to you and my shipmates. I guess I was not cut out for this line of work.

The legal officer adds, "Mr. Rawlings, your input will be important to the board of inquiry. I recommend you retain counsel."

To Rawlings, the word *counsel* sunk in. "Aye, Commander, and who will represent those WWII torn up crypto bags, the bags with holes in them, some with open seams? How about those metal fasteners that would not fasten, even though they were crypto cleared? In the past, those bags leaked like a sieve when we loaded them to carry material back from COMSEC. We had brand-new bags in the bos'un locker waiting to be made crypto ready, while being queued behind rope decorations for railings and ladders on captain gigs and admiral barges!"

Chief-of-Staff, "That's enough, Mr. Rawlings! You're out of order. Return to the crypto room. Mr. Sharp made a mess of the place while looking for the lost material. Get the room shipshape. Complete the inventory and have the alternate system going before we sail."

Ensign Rawlings did as ordered. Before the ship sailed from Subic Bay, he and Chief Jameson began reordering the crypto room that Sharp had disordered, folding the crypto bags for future use and placing them in their proper storage.

Rawlings' mind was on Mac's behavior. It made no sense. The loss of crypto keys was far from a death knell for a navy task force: Just send a broadcast message in the clear about the possible breach, and load a predetermined backup set of keys. The only question was if the new crypto channel was compromised. Thus, it was never used and the ongoing system provided adequate protection.

As Chief Jameson was folding up the last bag for stowage on an upper shelf, a set of crypto keys fell from the bag and tumbled to the deck. The stiff folds of a twenty-five-year-old piece of rotten canvas—approved for the transport of cryptographic material—had fulfilled its purpose: It delivered its contents, if a bit too late.

As they say, you go to war with what you have, including LTJG Sharp.

A symbolic burial at sea was held a few days later. Symbolic, in that Mr. Sharp was never found.

Before long, scuttlebutt around the fleet revealed the information that was transmitted to the Admiral, Western Pacific Amphibious Forces was from naval intelligence in Washington. It became obvious the needless sortie was politically, not militarily, motivated.

The message ordered the amphibious force to deploy with all possible speed to the waters off Saigon. There, the task force sailed around in circles for 60 days, waiting for a South Vietnamese coup of its top leader; a coup that was "known" to be imminent, but did not occur for many weeks.

CHAPTER 24

THE JUNK JUNKIES ROAD SHOW

One person's junk pile is another person's storage locker.
—anon

*A*nnouncer: "Welcome to another Junk Junkies Road Show, which is dedicated to the displaying and evaluating of America's junk. This junk is brought to our show by junk junkies, folks who are addicted to collecting discarded debris.

"We are doing today's program in an unusual locale: Beijing, China. Much of America's garbage is shipped to China and dumped in that country, so why not go to the source of so much junk! We want to thank China for its generosity of being America's junkyard.[8] Besides, it is amazing how much priceless junk can be retrieved from garbage."

First Exhibit: Used Bottle Caps

Antique (aka junk) vendor, hereafter referred to as Dealer, "Thank you for bringing in your soda pop bottle cap

---

[8] China has announced it will no longer accept America's trash, which has created turmoil in Uncle Sam's trash industry. One approach is to conduct more junk road shows, thus recycling the trash back to its originators.

collection—and all the way from America! Give us some history on the collection."

Owner of the collection, "Many years ago, my grandfather started the collection when he was a child. His first collection was earthworms, but they required a lot of dirt, and his mother grew tired of cleaning the boy's bedroom floor that had worms crawling around in piles of wet muck. Besides, his collection kept dying out on him, and his mom was also not fond of sweeping-up rotting worms.

"He abandoned earth worm collecting. He grew disappointed when they did not reciprocate his gentle stokes on their backs—not one lick of returned affection. So, he later moved to collecting marbles, but he was a poor shooter and eventually lost his marbles."

Dealer, "Hm. Interesting. Sorry about those dead worms and lost marbles, they would have been stellar exhibits for our show. But what about the bottle caps?"

Owner, "Oh yes, after losing all his marbles, my grandfather discovered none of the other kids collected caps from soda pop bottles. He had no competition and was able to collect the caps you see in this collection, all with little effort."

Dealer, "Ah! 'With little effort' is a big factor in the Junk Junkies Road Show. The less effort an owner has expended in acquiring a collection is a major factor in junk dealers raising the value of an object. Little effort, such as accidentally finding a piece of junk in an attic raises the price of the object a great deal. It makes for a more interesting story than actually expending effort in shopping for junk.

"As for your grandfather, his effort to collect earthworms entailed considerable work on his part. Sorry, but I must say that the long term prospect for his collection was a can of worms."

The Dealer continues, "How did your grandfather come

into the possession of so many soda bottle caps? There are hundreds in this collection."

Owner, "Collecting the caps became an obsession with granddaddy. He would prowl different stores looking for an unusual soda pop, buy the soda, drink it, and save the soda's bottle top cap."

"What happened to your grandfather?"

"He died of sugar diabetes at a young age. That's the price one sometimes pays for one's passion. Grandma put his collection in the basement of their home many years ago. Recently, I came across the bottle caps while searching for what remained of my marbles."

Dealer, "What you have is a truly unique collection, perhaps one of a kind. Ordinarily, a deranged junk junkie would cough-up $10,000 for this collection. However, the collection is missing a Nesbitt Orange soda bottle cap."

Owner, "Not so! There it is."

Dealer, "Yes, but it is not the bottle top cap from the original Nesbitt Orange product. It's one from a more recent bottle. You see, it does not have the cork inside the cap. If you can locate an original, and also show it was from a bottle that was opened—the cap must be bent and rusty—the $10,000 price should hold-up in a junk show auction.

"Otherwise, as of now, we cannot put a value on it. But antique worm collections! They are worth their weight in gold, even if their flimsy bodies are weightless. And a marble collection is worth its weight in having one of the treasured marbles in the collection.

"For example, an 'End of Day Onionskin marble' goes for $14,950."

Owner, "But it's essentially a piece of ordinary glass!"

Dealer, "Yes, but beauty is in the eyes of those who have lost their marbles."

Observation from announcer: If someone says to you, "You're losing your marbles," don't take offense. After all, they likely do not know you've already lost them.

Second Exhibit: Kermit's Signature

Dealer, "What you see here is a ceramic image of PBS's much beloved character, Kermit The Frog. Tell us, what brought you to this show with your Kermit sculpture?"

Owner, "First, let me say that I had trouble getting the piece through Chinese customs. They suspected I was actually starting a business that competed with their business."

Dealer, "Our staff is not aware the Chinese have a ceramic frog business."

Owner, "They didn't, but they do now."

Dealer, "Yes, more of that technology transfer situation. But today, we are dealing with lighter matters. So, what brings you to China to show us a ceramic image of a frog?"

"I wanted it to be examined and evaluated by an expert Kermit frog junk dealer."

Dealer, "You have come to the right place. This place is rife with ceramic frog specialists. First, let's examine the credentials of Kermit's image," as the Dealer carefully lays Kermit's ceramic body on its back, belly-side up.

"You can see," as the Dealer uses a precise and impressive looking pointer to expose tell-tell markings on Kermit's belly, "the subtle impressions into the stomach would leave a junk dealer to suspect this is not a replica of much value."

A silent observation from announcer: The owner of the Kermit ceramic has a vested interest in this discussion and evaluation. After all, the various markings on the bottoms, tops, and sides of potentially priceless (price-less?) treasures are what make this show a success.

The Dealer continues, "For example, consider a J.C. Penny

marking on the back of a dinner plate that is on exhibit at one of the shows here. It has George Washington's portrait on the front of it. It's one of millions of replications that were once sold at J.C. Penny's and placed on the tables and walls of millions of American kitchens. Who knows how many more of these patriotic plates still exist? One…Five…Thirty million?

"Furthermore, who could know what the idiosyncrasies of junk might reveal? Perhaps a cracked teacup from an obscure 17th century British duke might be worth nothing or thousands of dollars. Maybe a rare piece of correspondence from Donald Trump that has the word *humble* in it would be priceless—although in this example, we will never know. Or another Civil War bullet uncovered in the Gettysburg battlefield. Again, who knows?

"Anyway, notice the signature on the stomach of this replica of Kermit. It is signed 'Kermit the Frog.' That is not good news for you.

"PBS historians know that Kermit's puppet master always signed his name as 'Kermit *The* Frog.' The upper case "T" helped boost Kermit's reputation. A proper noun, instead of a mere lower case 'the'."

Owner, "But Kermit himself did not create this ceramic piece. An artist did."

Dealer, "Yes, but to be frank, it was from a less than competent and knowledgeable artist. Any ceramic artist worth his clay knows Kermit's middle name is a proper noun. How did you come into possession of this piece?"

"At a yard sale."

"What did you pay for it?"

"Twenty dollars."

Dealer, "The Kermit The Frog ceramic experts estimate your piece Kermit the Frog would go at an auction for…well, you might be able to give it away."

Third Exhibit: A Minute-by-Minute Watch

Owner, "I have brought in the pocket watch of my grandfather. Our family thinks its age makes for a valuable antique."

The Dealer begins his examination of the exhibit, "The watch was mass produced by a factory in Japan just after WWII. Notice the 'Made in occupied Japan' inscription on the back of the watch. In those days, these words branded a product as being inferior. Of course, Japan is no longer occupied and is producing superior products."

The Dealer continues his evaluation, "The glass on the face of the watch is cracked. The watch chain is rusted. Perfect for this road show!

"One more observation: The hour hand is missing."

Owner, "Yeah, and the watch is still working! Notice that the minute hand is still moving around just fine. I timed the minute hand with that of another watch. My granddad's minute hand is accurate to the second!"

Dealer, "We suggest you have your watch exhibited at the 'Time is Relative' auction show being held in Los Angeles next week. The auction exhibits clocks and watches that are broken or not ticking just right, along with several of Albert Einstein's reverse winding clocks. Your watch might be a real winner there. It tells time, but does not tell time.

"By the way, the Time is Relative auction is a subsidiary of The Junk Junkies Road Show."

Announcer: "There you have it for another road show for junk yard junkies. Next week, we'll be back in America to examine another All American junk filled city. And don't forget our motto, "What a piece of junk is to one, is an antique to another."

CHAPTER 25

THE SPOILS OF WAR

*C*hief Petty Officer of a single helicopter flight deck, "Good hunting, sir?"

Frank, the pilot, "Damned good hunting, Chief."

"Spot anything?"

"Yeah. Amazing. It's only my second sortie since I came aboard the ship, and I flew over another cache about a mile inland from where we're cruising. Two recons, two likely Charlie sites. Before reporting to this rust bucket of a ship, my briefings on the carrier were off base. Intel has no clue what Charlie's doing in this area."

"One mile's pretty close to our patrols, sir. Charlie's up to something. Our reconnaissance has not spotted any sites around that area. They must be new."

"Yeah, and I'll give'em credit. It takes some balls to set up a village from scratch that close to our patrols, but that looks like what they've done. They're getting bolder Chief, but we'll find 'em.

"Still this one was not easy to spot. I couldn't see it 'till I was nearly clipping the trees. Anyway, I'd wager it's another

Viet Cong staging point. Not many men around, probably a place for Charlie to store supplies."

"You got a lot of detail, sir. You must'a had some clear views with good weather. It's unusual for Charlie to expose his sites."

"I landed on site to check the place out."

"Sir, you landed!"

"Yeah, I put myself down, smack in the middle of the town square, so to speak. No guts, no air medals. As I said, not any men present, except for a few old ones. Seemed safe enough. I idled the engine, got out and looked around, .45 in hand. People scattered away from my bird like scared rats.

"Before I forget, I'm still worried about the gas gauge, Chief. The needle showed full, then half-full, then full. I can't get a good reading.

"Anyway, there's not much to be seen by flying over these villages. Everything's buried in caves and tunnels: rifles, grenades, ammo. But we're onto their tricks. I'll tell intel to send-in some raids in those areas."

Chief, "Yes sir. By the way, the frogmen on our ship snared two men carrying explosives outside a village southwest of where you've been flying."

"Did we get any intel out of them?

"Wouldn't know, sir. Not cleared. No need to know."

"Okay, I'll check with the intel officers. Maybe they can give me better information than the carrier guys did.

"I've made some notes for intel. Didn't land at the first site, but I came across a tunnel entrance in the second site. I looked around the area a bit. Didn't go inside the tunnel. Not that stupid.

"Anyway, the villagers looked like they'd seen a ghost! First time they'd seen a chopper up close, I'd bet. Most of them high-tailed it into the bushes. I took a few souvenirs. And here I am. No worse for wear."

"Sir, about that landing. The mission for our recons is to do fly overs. We've got the special forces and SEALs to go inland based on our recon. They're tunnel dogs. That's their job. Sir, don't risk... "

"The mission is surveillance and reconnaissance. Chief, were you in the briefing room on the carrier? Where are you going with this mission fly over crap? Keep my bird going, that's your job. I determine where the chopper goes."

"Aye, sir, sorry. We'll secure the Cayuse and have it ready shortly. (See postscript.) Are you going out again today?"

"Yeah, making hay while the sun shines. Have the 'chopper' ready by 1500."

"Aye, sir. Eh, just curious. Since you were already on the ground, did you spot many younger men in that hamlet?"

"Aren't you listening, Chief"? Just old men, but I decided I had best get moving along, and that's that.

"No more questions, Chief. It's not your place to question an officer. By the way, I looked at your file when I came aboard last night. The clerk told me you're married to a local. That true?"

"It is, sir. About ten years ago, I was a first class petty officer, billeted at a navy post in Saigon after the French Dien Bien Phu surrender. We were stationed there to help the French clean up their mess. I'm pretty good with engines and was assigned to the motor pool. I guess that's one reason I'm the head of the flight deck on this recon ship. Okay, this assignment is only my second class petty officer and me, but we only have one helo on this ship to tend to.

"Anyway, sir, I met her at a reception at the French legation. I was on duty as an honor guard for the evening. She was a guest and came over to talk to me. Completely floored me! This beautiful woman, picking a swabee to talk to. Been with her ever since."

"Not a downtown pickup? That's pretty strange. Never came across a slant-eye who didn't go down for a dollar or two."

…"Mr. Rawlings, I'm not sure if you are referring to my wife. If you are, with respect to an officer, you're off base, regardless of your rank. I met her at the legation. I did not meet her downtown at a bar. She comes from a prominent family who live in Hue. They're likely more prominent than yours or mine."

"Okay, keep you dander down, Chief. Anyway, downtown, uptown, whatever. Out here in Vietnam, looks like you and your honey are in a family feud: slant-eyes versus round-eyes. That's the facts, Chief, regardless of your comeuppance. Anyway, I'll be back after chow. Make sure you check the gas gauge."

"It will be taken care of, Mr. Rawlings. Petty Officer Smith and I team up to do the pre-flight check and oversee all maintenance. I know my one-chopper flight deck is not what you have on the carrier, but I'll take care of the bird.

"Besides, the gas gauge is working, sir. Before your last flight, I rechecked the fuel line and the tank while Smith rechecked the cockpit panel. It's part of our routine."

"It's not accurate, Chief. Enough said? Fix it!"

"Will do, lieutenant."

"Okay, and don't get bent out of shape about my bringing up your wife being downtown. I've never come across an Asian woman that didn't hang around our liberty ports, looking for a drunk sailor to rob. They have hinges on their heels. They lie down for a couple bucks, then steal the sailor's loot while he's sleeping. I'm not very fond of them."

"I gathered as much. I'll keep that in mind."

"Good. I'm headed for some chow. Time to meet my new mess mates."

***

Frank, "Gentlemen, I'm glad to be assigned to this ship and to be part of this wardroom. I've just filed the details of my first two flight recons with Dan and his spooks. Two sorties, two probable finds. I've located two places in need of serious incursion."

Dan, an intelligence officer: "Stow it, Frank. You're new here. We have only a few officers cleared for this type of intel. Officer's mess is not the place for this conversation."

"Lighten up, Dan. Just having a joke. I'll wager your intel guys will back my reports. Anyway, just between us, here's a bit of unclassified scuttlebutt from yours truly. I bring up the subject so we can form, well, maybe a partnership. I can't do it alone."

"Do what, Frank?"

Frank, "Selling souvenirs. Gentlemen, that land you see just a short distance from this ship is a take-all-you-want museum of junk. But it's expensive junk to American museums, to anyone who just wants Vietnam War souvenirs, and especially to collectors. There's a free shopping center for all of us, and it's within reach."

Dan, "Listen, Frank, everyone knows there were all kinds of stuff in Vietnam that could be bought for almost nothing. I've got a buddy that's assigned to MACV in Saigon. For a while, he shopped around and got some good bargains. He made a killing in San Diego by selling rolls of elephant skin. Had a pair of golf shoes and wallets made from some of the hide. Now, there are too many Americans. Prices have gone up; not a lot of shopping unless you're talking about trinkets."

"Yeah, I know, but this ship is not sailing near Saigon. We're up the coast. And this area has had no American military unit stationed nearby. Think of it! There's stuff in those villages that's worth a lot of money. It's junk to its owners, but it can bring in some loot back in the states.

Dan, "Sounds good in theory, but we're sea locked here. We can't get ashore to buy anything. We can't even get anything for our wives. We had liberty last month in Hong Kong, but so did half the Seventh Fleet. Other than hand-made suits and cameras, it was just more variations of fish and rice for dinner.

"We're not allowed to go ashore. Maybe we never will hit land in this area. Our intelligence on this part of the coast comes from the Cayuse program and the SEALs' surveys. From the dispatches we monitor out of Hawaii, our crew won't see land, and we won't have liberty until the Marines secure some beaches near a large city, like Danang. Who knows when that will be? We may be back on the west coast by then. Right, Ted?"

Ted, "Yep. Six months in the South China Sea. Recon duty to look for enemy supply bases and camps. No land, no liberty."

Frank, "That's your problem, swabees. You should have gone airborne. Look, Dan, Ted—all of you in this ward-room—my chopper and I are doing the work the frogmen we got aboard should be doing. They can't see beyond their face masks. All they do is beach recon, maybe a few yards inland for a raid.

"Beaches? Play it back, Sam: WWII and Normandy. The action's gonna' be inland, where I go. By the way, where are the froggies today?"

"They captured two Charlies, so they must be doing some-thing right. And they're doing a beach survey today. It might come in handy if special forces have to beach their boats for a raid on those supply bases. 'Course you wouldn't know about that, coming from the airdale world."

Dan continues, "What's with you, Frank? To acquaint you with the real Navy, flyboy, we're not swabees. We're United States Navy officers, serving aboard a United States naval ship."

Frank, "Ha! Don't get so upset over nothing. But the truth is, I feel sorry for you. Come on! This World War II tub is a cork on the sea. You won't even make it back to San Diego until another World War II relic is raised from the graveyard and sent to relieve you. Raise your heights, even in these low seas."

Dan, "We have no idea what you're talking about. Man, you spew more BS than most flyboys, and that's saying something."

Frank, "Gentlemen, with all respect, you are pedestrians! Consider this: It will be a long time before you go ashore in Vietnam. Maybe never. The way things are going in Washington, you'll be back in San Diego with your missus before you have a chance for any fighting, much less, R&R. You'll get a Vietnam campaign battle ribbon for never having set one foot in Vietnam.

"In the meantime, I'll give you an idea of what you might experience. I'm bringing back souvenirs from the shore. I'm putting them up for sale to the members of this wardroom. Exclusive deal, gents! Even if you don't land in Vietnam, you can convince anyone to believe you *were* in Vietnam. What do they need to know anyway? A campaign ribbon on your chest you can show to…well, who cares!

"I'm making two to three flights a day. My small bird can light down almost anywhere. I'll do my recon, and I'll pick up some artifacts. Just think! No one like us has ever been in this area. Gentlemen, it's virgin territory, in more ways than one.

"There's stuff in those villages that'll sell like hell in the states. I can easily bring it onboard, but I can't stow all of it.

So, piece of cake, I sell some of it to you on the cheap. You can take it home, sell it to museums, art collectors. Gentlemen, you can make a bundle of money."

Dan, "Big deal. What's a straw hat worth?"

"Good question. Look. Here's a coin I got from a peasant at the site where I landed this morning. I've got other coins in my helo. There's a mint out there.

"I'm not a coin collector but this coin—look at it—it's as big as my hand. It's ancient, gotta' be worth a lot."

Ted, "How'd you get it? Our other pilots from the carrier never talked about landing. It was always low level reconnaissance. "

"Well, I did land. To your question, I made an old woman an offer she couldn't refuse.

"So, who wants to buy this coin? Make yourself some loot. And I'm flying out to get more stuff this afternoon. Okay, gentlemen, I'm taking bids for this one. I'll bring in more booty at evening mess.

…"Okay, swabees. It'll be your loss and my gain. I'll unload them on our R&R stop in Hong Kong. British tourists will love them."

* * *

"Hey, Chief, come here."

"What's up, Smith?"

"I found this sack behind the pilot's seat."

"Damn! It's ancient Vietnam money! We have one of those kinds of coins at home. My wife has placed it on our mantel. She got it from her grandfather, who got it from his family. She says it goes back to the early 1800s. It's a family heirloom."

"What's a coin like this worth, Chief?"

Chief, "Depends on its condition, and especially if it's one of the rare ones. If it is, it's worth a lot."

Smith, "What are they doing in the helo? And look, there's blood on some of those coins and some on the sack. It's still wet. What the… ."

"…Fortunes of war, Smith. We're in a combat zone."

Smith, "Chief, I listened to your conversation with the pilot earlier, and even I know he ain't supposed to be landing. And he's sure as hell's not supposed to be target shooting. He's recon only, Chief."

"I didn't attend his briefings when he was aboard the carrier before coming aboard here. Did you?"

"No, but… "

"Smith, this is officer business. Not only is he an officer, he's Intel. We're deck hands. We keep our noses out of it, and we keep our noses clean. Babbling about blood and those coins inside the chopper could lead to our getting in trouble for messing around with intel material."

"Aye, Chief."

"You bet your ass, 'Aye,' and mine, too, Smith. I'd get the rap, as well as you. Forget what you saw. This is intelligence material, probably classified. You never should have looked in that sack. Put it back where you found it. This conversation is over and never to be brought up again. Ever! Savvy?"

"Sorry, Chief. My mistake, thanks."

"Finish the panel check. I'll take another look at the gas line. Stay in the cockpit and give me a reading on the gauge."

* * *

"Chief, the gauge shows full."

"Very well. Go get us some food, chow line's going to close soon. Hurry it up, and bring me a sandwich and some coffee."

"Damn straight, Chief. And thanks again about that sack of coins. My lips are sealed."

THE SPOILS OF WAR

Frank, "Not bad chow for a rust bucket. Can't say the same for my new mess mates. Not too friendly. Did you fix the gas gauge?"

Chief, "Yes. I've taken care of the problem."

Frank, "Good. It had better be fixed, or you'll catch hell on my return."

Chief, "I am positive you will not be giving me hell, sir."

* * *

Dan, in the officers' mess, "Well, so much for fame and fortune."

Another officer, "He was an ass to begin with."

Yet another, "Yeah, but a harmless ass."

"Think so?"

"Yeah. Bravado BS stuff, not like the other airdales we've had aboard. That coin he wanted to sell us, how many could he possibly find? Same goes for anything that's in the villages. Saigon is where the money is, or was."

"What's with the recovery of his chopper?"

"Not much to recover. The Cayuse was totaled. A couple choppers from the carrier flew in, but the foliage and trees restricted much of a salvage operation. So, they roped him up along with the flight log into one of the choppers and torched the wreck. His body is on the carrier. They sent a message to have our stewards bundle up his personal effects from his wardroom. The replacement Cayuse will ferry his stuff back to the carrier."

"Wonder what happened to those coins he said he had on the helo?"

"Probably still there, along with the coin he tried to stick us with. Hey, Dan, pass the potatoes."

Postscript

The OH-6A Cayuse was a small tactical helicopter. During the early years of the Vietnam War, it was deployed on out-fitted decks of small ships and on pre-built platforms of larger WWII vessels to fly reconnaissance missions. In those early days, many of these missions were of an ad-hoc nature.[9] One such craft was assigned to a ship on which I was deployed.

---

[9] Photograph is sourced from keying in "Small Helicopters used in Vietnam War."

THE SPOILS OF WAR

CHAPTER 26

FLORAL INFANTICIDE

his was the year he was going to pitch in and help his wife with the shrubbery, trees, and lawns surrounding their home. For the first time in their marriage, he took on the task of helping with his wife's treasured foliage.

It was not as if he were a domestic demagogue who kept his mate tied to yard work. He offered to hire landscaping people with his vow: Let others tend to the outside, that's not where Netflix is located.

She was of the opposite nature. She loved her pastime in the yard. With the exception of mowing and tree removal, his wife took care of their outdoors. She even liked trimming the edges of the lawn.

It was not exactly one-sided, as she informed him on occasion, "I'm in the yard today, honey. You're turn at the stove." Fair enough for him. Hamburger Helper had many variations.

The main task delegated to him by the yard warden was killing the undesirable species of plant life, and fending off predatory deer from having their favorite meal in the yard: flowers. She identified the unwanted plants to be pulled from the ground or sprayed. They all looked alike to him. However, by venturing outdoors on occasion to perform the obligatory backyard barbeque, he had no trouble identifying a deer.

Thus, his wife did most of the horticulture around their home, as these tasks required some skill. He kept the house exterior in shape but he himself was not tasked with preventative maintenance. He hired painters and carpenters to keep their home ship shape, and others to prune and remove trees. At this time in his later years, he had unashamedly taken on the role of a 21st century couch potato.

His mate also took on the job of planting newly purchased plants, which required a more refined green thumb than her husband possessed. During this one spring, she decided to redo much of the back yard. In preparation, she purchased 100 pots of plants and flowers.

Upon bringing the pots home from the store, she had to leave town unexpectedly on a four-day family trip. Before departing, her husband was instructed to buy ample supplies of floral poison and apply it to places in which rogue grass, weeds, and dandelions were sneaking up on innocent plant life. Once again, she provided a tutorial on the good guy and the bad guy plants.

Because the newly purchased plants and flowers were still in their pots in the back yard, and the nearby marauding deer were salivating (if deer can salivate), the husband was given several additional tasks: "Go to the local nursery and purchase my favorite fertilizer spray for the new plants and flowers. Water the newcomers today and two days hence. Buy more weed killer and deer repellant. Apply the spray fertilizer and deer repellant to the new flowers and plants as soon as

FLORAL INFANTICIDE

possible. Re-spray the weeds and dandelions. I can't seem to control them."

Having delegated her floral authority to her lieutenant, she left for California, and he departed to the local nursery to purchase plant killer spray, deer repellant, and fertilizer.

But before he left the back yard, he spotted the deer scouting team. Standing at the periphery to his yard, they had detected their next meal. He was the only line of defense. Round trip, the nursery was an hour away. One-hundred pots of assorted vegetation would be one-hundred pots of dug-up dirt on his return.

Ring, ring. "Hello, Smith residence."

"Jim, this is Hank. Need a favor. Could you come over to my backyard? Got a bit of an emergency here."

"Sure, what's the problem?"

"I need you to stand guard on one-hundred pots of flowers and plants while I go to the nursery to pick up some of Helen's favorite sprays for flowers and plants."

"Deer?"

"Yeah, they're already circling the wagons."

"Been there, done that. Be right over."

The homeowner in this story was little versed on matters of the soil. While his wife labored outdoors, he labored indoors, a role reversal that had their neighbors joke with them about their swapping some conventional domestic duties of man and wife.

Thus, he knew about spray bottles that contained cleaning and polishing products. His many sessions in the kitchen had taught him well. He was amazed by the number of spray bottles consumers unwittingly purchased that refused to spray forth their contents. Some of the nozzles on the bottles were adjustable to supposedly spray a concentrated stream of the liquid or a finer mist. One such product sprayed nothing or if set to the next option, produced a pathetic dribble of droplets.

For the task at hand, he took no chances on the bottles he was buying at the nursery. He purchased several empty sprayer bottles. In the past, he had success buying this brand, as they actually sprayed! It was somewhat of a luxurious purchase, but with his newly appointed responsibilities from the Captain of the Garden Guard, he was not going to take a chance of returning home with underperforming spray bottles.

Any job worth doing was worth doing well. Besides, he would be tending to one of his wife's favorite hobbies. …She had two green thumbs.

With his wife's unexpected departure, he suddenly found himself with scores of infant flowers in his care. Their health depended on the application of fertilizer and deer repellent. Plus, those dandelions were getting out of hand.

The deer visiting their home seemed to be made up of Nazi storm troopers that made regular raids on their yard. They appeared to post sentries around his lawn and shrubbery. He could have sworn the sentries' job was to signal to their comrades when any new flora had arrived. Unless a person was physically present or a noxious chemical was in the air, the other deer would immediately leave their nearby bivouac to attack the plants. They always honed in on the newest plantings and took no prisoners.

He was well aware he needed to protect his wife's baby plants as soon as possible.

Because of his expertise with sprayer bottles, he did not bother testing the sprayers on the purchased bottles at the nursery. He bought several of his preferred (empty) bottles and intended to enter into a spraying program upon returning home. He expected the specialized sprayers to outperform the wannabes; hence, the direct use of his preferred brand of sprayer. When in a bind, go with the best. The result was the transfer of the liquids into the recently purchased proven high-powered sprayers.

While he was at it, and at his wife's directions, while spending this time in the back yard, he would kill two birds with one stone. He would also re-spray those damned weeds. Good thing he bought extra spray bottles.

As he completed pouring the liquids into the generic bottles, a phone call came in. The call required he return to his office to log onto the Internet. That he did, and there he remained for few minutes. When he hurriedly returned to his spraying task, it was nearing darkness. Luckily, the deer had been marauding a neighbor's pansies and not yet eaten any of his wife's flowering one-hundred.

He picked up the fertilizer bottle first and sprayed the newly purchased flowers. For good measure, he sprayed other plants around the yard. Next, he applied the deer repellent over most of the back yard. Using the remaining light, he finished the yard tasks for the day by spraying the plant killer liquid on the villain flora. All was well. Tomorrow, he would safely plant 100 new arrivals to their backyard.

A couple days later, he noticed the new plants were dying. Not one, not two, all of them. How could that be? Yet the nearby dandelions were in their height of glory.

No! Could he have used the wrong bottles on the flowers? Could he have put plant killer on the flowers and plant redeemer on the dandelions and weeds?

Nearing panic, he ran into the garage to recheck the bottles. Because of the interruption a couple days before, he had not taken the time to label the new bottles. Their contents were almost identical in looks: a semi-thick creamy liquid, slightly brown. Upon examination, he could not tell them apart and tried to remember the applications he made a couple days ago.

On the early evening of their first use, after the Internet session, he had assumed a killer bottle was to the right as he faced it, and a savior bottle was to his left. Now, after inspecting the two, he realized he had mixed them up, and had spent his time devoutly doing his duty with the wrong bottle in hand. He had committed floral infanticide. To compound his problems, he had protected rogue flora. Reverse ethnic floral cleansing.

Surprised and disgusted, he knew he had to fix matters, especially before the yard warden returned from her trip. Consulting with his neighbor again, he then hurried back to the nursery. Several metal racks held an assortment of infant flowers, but the pickings were few.

He asked the cashier, "Any more flowers than those on the rack?"

"For now, no. It's been a busy week. New shipment is due in two days."

He didn't have two days to waste, "I'll take most of what you have in the racks."

"Great! I'll have someone give you a hand."

He was met at the flower racks by a clerk, "Which ones do you want?"

"I need about one-hundred pots of…whatever."

"You must have a new yard (an understatement). I'll load'um up. You might need to take two trips."

"Yeah, and load up ten bags of soil and five bags of fertilizer."

He chose any flower with colorful petals. He was desperate, any color in a storm. He had the clerk put them in his vehicle, paid for them, made two trips back to the house to: (a) dig up the dead bodies around the yard, (b) remove the poisoned soil that had surrounded them, (c) refurbish the holes with fresh soil and fertilizer, (d) begin the replanting, (e) contribute two-hundred empty flower pots to a bewildered Good Will truck employee, and (f) encounter two successive days of heavy and constant rain. The backyard was flooded, so were the new plants.

True to the old saying, "Past shame, past grace," he came clean with a call to his wife. He explained the massacre, his plans for the reincarnation, and how the weather had stymied his noble intentions. She seemed aloof to his plight, merely asking what kinds of flowers he had purchased. His reply of, "mostly reds, purples, and blues" brought forth silence. He learned his purchases were not what she had in mind, but he was not aware of this deficiency until she returned from her trip.

In assessing the final damage, he discovered he had assassinated not only 100 new plants, but scores of his wife's prized Primroses. They had once graced the perimeter of one of her favorite flower beds. He was guilty of more than floral infanticide, he was also the liquidator of adults.

After silently strolling through the back yard, his wife stoically stated, "I'll take care of the situation." As his eyes glazed over, she explained his selections did not meet the needs of the yard in relation to perennials, annuals, deciduous, and other unfathomable categories of plants.

She then used a marker to label his generic bottles and handed them to him. He took this last action to mean that in spite of his sin, he had not been banned from performing limited garden work. Maybe he was banned from the Garden of Eden for a while, but not the garden in the backyard.

CHAPTER 27

THE WHIP

The child was playing in the lamb barn, a wooden enclosure used to protect newly born sheep from the harsh weather of America's southwest high plains. Except for the boy and the wooden lily pads he had placed in the metal water tank, the large barn was empty. The sheep births would come later in the year.

At that time, the boy would join his father, brothers, and hired hands to sort out those sheep in need of care. Their job was to make sure the soon-to-be mothers were out of the weather and later, properly positioned to present their nascent lambs to the world.

The lamb barn was more than a sanctuary for sheep. The child also used the enclosure to protect and nurture tadpoles. After a rare rain shower, large puddles of rapidly evaporating water began to yield to the sun and the desiccated soil. Thousands of soon-to-be frogs vied among themselves for access to the receding water in the puddle. The tiny amphibians were racing against time.

The child attempted to support their quest for survival by scooping them from their ponds into a bucket. He then transported them to the tank in the lamb barn. He knew nothing about how a tadpole went about becoming a frog. But he was sure of one thing: The soon-to-be frogs needed a way to leave the metal tank. Thus, he created the wooden lily pads. He was not certain his invention led to the tank becoming empty of frogs, but he was happy that his amphibious companions were now somewhere else.

It was during his placing of the frogs' launching pads into the tank that a familiar sound came from the side of the barn that fronted the main yard of the ranch complex: The crack of a bull whip and the painful neighing of a horse.

The lad knew his father was once again confronting his favorite quarter horse stud. Stated another way, the lad knew the horse was once again confronting its owner. The boy, scared at what he was to behold, yet transfixed at the same time, left the sheep barn and walked slowly onto the main driving area facing the house. There, in an attempt to coerce the stud to enter into a trailer, he once again saw his father applying a bull whip to the horse.

Wack! "Get in there you son of a bitch!" Wack!

The horse, tied with his halter to the front of the trailer's interior, neighed in pain and protest, but would not move an inch.

Wack! "You son of a bitch!" Wack!

The child grew nauseous. He wished to retreat to his tank of tadpoles. He wished to rush to his father, to entreat him to put down the bull whip. But he was afraid. He was afraid of his father. He was afraid of the stud.

He stood still, just a few feet from the beating, half-sick with disgust, but fearful of what he was witnessing. He was ashamed of himself for his lack of courage to step in and ashamed at his father for his cruelty. His father had never laid a hand on him. His dual personality confounded the child.

His father finally gave up. In revulsion, perhaps at himself, the man threw the bull whip to the ground and walked away from the horse. Bleeding from its back and hindquarters—positioned at the end of the trailer, the stud silently stood his ground. The father disappeared into the house.

Shortly thereafter, the child's big brother emerged from the house. Who knows what transpired between the father and the big brother? Likely nothing, but the brother knew this horse, and this horse knew the brother. As well, the brother knew what had gone on in the main yard, but he also knew to stay away from his father when the elder man was in a lather.

The younger child's guilt was somewhat assuaged. If his older brother would not challenge his father, how could he?

Still shaken, the child stood in his place. He watched his older brother walk to the back of the trailer. The brother stood there for a while, looking at the horse, while the horse looked at him. After a moment or so, he placed his hand on the top of the horse's head and ears, a normally untouchable part of a horse's anatomy—at least for strangers.

The brother breathed into the nostrils of the horse. The horse breathed back. The brother patted the neck and chest of the horse, while continuing to breathe with the horse. The brother untied the halter from the trailer and walked the stud into the trailer.

The brother closed the trailer gate and walked back to the house. Shortly, the father came from the house, entered the pickup, which pulled the trailer and horse from the main yard.

The boy returned to his tadpole tank. The bull whip remained on the ground.

CHAPTER 28

SAN ANTONIO ROSE
AND MOONLIGHT SONATA

The bar at an expensive hotel was full of customers. The time was late evening, not yet midnight, but close. A man seated at a baby grand piano was pounding out tunes of the 1940s and '50s. Nearby, a small dance floor grudgingly accommodated its patrons, as they danced to the old standbys. It was a typical Saturday night at an upscale piano lounge.

It appeared the evening's music was to be the standard fare. But after a while, a recurrent set of chords caught the patrons' ears. Altered only by the rhythm of different dance steps, the pianist had begun playing the same melody time and again: "San Antonio Rose."

Foxtrots, waltzes, sambas, and mambos, all to the tune of the famous Texas song. Some of the dancers looked askance at the piano player. Most kept dancing, likely wondering why he had chosen such eclectic renditions of a song. But music was music. The crowd was high and highly festive.

Next to the piano sat several men, who were a bit raucous and a bit high. All had Texas style hats on their heads, oblivious to other customers, many who were dressed in east coast evening wear. Some were in tuxedoes and evening gowns, having just attended a classical music program at a nearby concert hall.

The reason for the pianist playing the recurring Texas melody was soon discovered. A man was placing a one-hundred dollar bill on the piano each time "San Antonio Rose" was played. This man belonged to a table occupied by the six Texans. They were dictating the musical menu for the evening.

After the conclusion of one of the tunes, the men would take turns opening their wallets, passing the bill to their designated donor, who would semi-stagger to the piano and place the bill directly on the keyboard, just in case the pianist might miss its presence. He would then request, "Play San Antonio Rose one more time." An offer the piano player could hardly refuse.

The crowd in the lounge soon caught on to the bribes. "My god, look at those one-hundred dollar bills!" No one cared; just the opposite. The music, the Texans, and the one-hundred dollar bills made for amusing entertainment. It beat the ponderous classical fare heard earlier at the concert hall.

The piano player was especially pleased. He improvised "San Antonio Rose" scores as if there were no tomorrow, at least a tomorrow no longer populated with generous, drunk Texans. It is likely more than one person in the lounge wished they had taken piano lessons as a child.

In the spirit of the evening, the elation of the pianist and the drunk Texans, more couples joined the already crowded dance floor. The assemblage resembled a troupe of Keystone

Cops with the dancers trying to keep step to a "San Antonio Rose" rumba.

The piano player took a break. The patrons watched him gather up his newly found wealth. He expressed gratitude to his audience, especially the Texans: "I thank all of you. This is the most fun I have ever had playing at a lounge. I especially want to thank my Texas friends!"

From the audience came an anonymous challenge, "How do you know they're Texans?"

As the pianist exited the lounge for his break, he responded, "Because not once did they ask me to play 'Oklahoma'."

He exited the room, most likely destined for the hotel safe or a bank deposit kiosk.

After the pianist was gone, the room remained a lively assemblage of revelers, all caught up in conversations at their tables. The absence of music lent an air of aural relief to the lounge.

The musical interlude at the bar settled into a hiatus in between what the patrons expected next and what the pianist hoped would be successive "San Antonio Rose" music sets.

At this time, a tuxedoed man left his seat from the rear of the lounge. He was recognized by several of the customers, as he had performed a piano solo during the earlier concert. "Say, remember him? He did that Chopin piece."

But few paid any attention to him until a few seconds later, when the lounge was once again filled with music. The tuxedoed man had seated himself at the piano and had begun playing Beethoven's "Moonlight Sonata."

The noise of the lounge pushed this music into an audible background—just faintly discernible to the ear. The people in the lounge were paying little or no attention to the new pianist. His music was competing with ongoing conversations and laughter.

But not for long. Gradually, the voices in the lounge became silent, as eyes turned toward the source of this plaintive, beautiful tune. Shortly thereafter, except for the piano music, the lounge was silent. Not a sound could be heard beyond Beethoven's masterpiece. No one was moving or speaking. Even the Texans were quiet. In less than one minute, the lounge had undergone a transformation from a boisterous bar to a subdued miniature concert hall.

"Moonlight Sonata" is not a long piece, running only a few minutes. But during that short time, the people in the bar shared an intimate experience. The common encounter of listening to the "Moonlight Sonata"—its abrupt, beautiful interruption into the evening—had bonded a small number of people together, if only for a brief time.

The pianist finished the piece, and without further ado, left his seat at the piano to return to his table and his friends. For a moment, his audience remained silent, still enthralled by the musical interlude.

Shortly, a smattering of applause could be heard coming from the Texans' table. The one-hundred dollar bill Texan stood up as he clapped, which led to most patrons joining in the applause, some also standing while they acclaimed the beautiful performance of one of their fellow bar patrons.

During this ovation, the pianist smiled a bit, bowed his head ever so slightly, then turned his attention to his friends.

Gradually, the room returned to its normal revelry. The talking and laughter increased to the Saturday night pre-scribed decibel levels. The lounge pianist returned to the piano for another set of music.

To his chagrin, and to the probable relief of everyone else in the room, he played no more versions of the "San Antonio Rose." Like Elvis, the Lone Star State citizens had left the building for the evening.

As an added bonus, the now absent Texans would not ask the concert pianist for a "San Antonio Rose" rendition of "Moonlight Sonata."

CHAPTER 29

OF LITTLE INTEREST[10]

*H*is retirement party preceded the loss of his retirement fund by a few months. The party was given by his family. He had been self employed but was prudent enough to save for later years. The party was a fitting celebration to his years of labor.

As a young man, he had signed on to an IRA, consisting of mutual funds, interspersed with few CDs. His IRA contents reflected his approach to life: Stay the course; dig in; persist. Keep going in order to protect his family against an unknown future. True to his nature, his savings were invested in modest and safe investments.

A few years ago, he had taken out a second mortgage on his home to help fund the retirement account. It was a sound move: putting his equity to work. His social security check would be ordinary, as he had brought in modest levels of income during his working years. His wife had stayed home

---

10   The statistics cited are sourced from *The Nearly Perfect Storm: A Financial and Social Failure*, by this writer and available at Amazon.com.

to raise their four children, who were now on their own. While taking in his retirement party, he was relieved. After years of work, years of ease lay ahead.

One modest luxury he could now afford was watching the early evening news. In the past, this news came on too early because he was still working. If he had the energy after a long day, he would sometimes stay up late to watch a rerun of the earlier broadcast. But now, he could take a morsel of satisfaction from his past labors: He could watch the Six O'clock News Hour at its designated time:

> On the financial scene tonight, the head of the International Monetary Fund stated the world's financial system was on the brink of a meltdown. The stock market reacted accordingly.

Within a few months, his IRA account was reduced by one-half. The CDs held firm for a while, but the renewal interest rates declined. The mutual funds plunged in value.

His children were not immune from the marketplace. They had purchased homes and were seeing their major investment wither. He learned from the news:

> In the nation's capital, the Federal Reserve stated that mortgage defaults in America increased by nearly 500 percent over the past 24 months. Home values are seeing their largest declines in decades. Presently, 26 percent of all homeowners in the United States have negative equity in their homes.

The value of his home and those of his children declined but their mortgage payments did not. Not being a well read man, he failed to understand the implications of a variable rate mortgage loan. But then, neither did those who were well read. The Six PM News informed him:

> *The New York Times* released its analysis of CEO compensation for seven large financial institutions, all of which have failed to perform the past two years. This compensation ranged from $49 million to $483 million paid out over the past nine years. These officers continue to receive multimillion dollar packages.

> On the local scene, a couple who bought their home two years ago discovered their monthly mortgage payment was increasing from $954 to $1320. The husband had recently been fired from a job he had held for ten years. His wife cannot work, as they have three young children.

Thus, this man's son, with his wife and three children, walked away from a $1,320 house payment. The path they took led to his doorstep. The trek was followed by his daughter, now unemployed and a former owner of an underwater mortgage.

What could he do? He could not close the door on his children. In the meantime, his mortgage payment had increased by 15 percent, a significant drain on his limited income.

His retirement was not what he had hoped for. It had begun with bright prospects. Now, it was one of muted despair. What had he done wrong? He had worked and saved. What else could he do? From the Six O'Clock News Hour, he learned:

> And in Washington, in order to give borrowers easier access to capital, the Federal Reserve will keep interest rates low for the foreseeable future. This marks the

OF LITTLE INTEREST

eighth successive year the Fed has held down interest rates.

His stocks were worth far less than what he had paid for them. His CDs' interest income was little more than an irritating entry on the monthly statement. Where could he go to gain leverage on his limited savings? If he were a borrower, he would be in financial heaven: cheap loans. But he was not, and with the exception of his mortgage, nor had he ever been.

He had followed the advice of Uncle Sam: save! And where were his savings? Gone with the stock market; gone with the CDs, now hapless, archaic instruments.

He made some rough calculations. If his CDs alone had paid out a modest 4 percent interest over the past eight years, he would have had a sufficient buffer to weather this storm. But they did not. His bank was paying no more than one percent on savings, yet his mortgage was over six percent. The early evening news provided another view on interest rates. He watched it with increasing despondency:

> In Washington today, the Federal Reserve announced the rate it charges banks to borrow money from the Fed will continue to be less than 0.75 percent. The Fed has kept this rate at less than 1.75 percent for several years. The Fed's motive is to make it easier for banks to obtain quick liquidity.

With children and grand children moving into his home, with his stocks and residence worth less than what he paid for them, with his fixed savings earning less than inflation, he found himself deficit spending. The realization of this stark fact set him back, not just financially but emotionally as well. For all he had done, for all he had worked for, it was coming to naught. With each passing month, he became poorer. The Six O'clock News Hour reported:

On the local front, an investigation into the vehicular death of a recent retiree has gone to the courts. The dead man's wife and children contend that the crash of his car into a concrete embankment was an accident and not a suicide. The man's insurance company has filed a counter claim that he had exhibited signs of remorse about his family's financial problems and had killed himself to pass the insurance payout to his wife and their four children. Currently, the lawsuit is still under litigation. We'll keep you updated.

Meanwhile, the economy continues to make strides toward recovery, evidenced by the quarterly bonuses paid out to banking and other financial executives.

OF LITTLE INTEREST

CHAPTER 30

THE BULL RIDER

*T*he boy's chores began at the break of dawn. A noisy rooster raised the child from his slumber. As he opened his eyes and looked around, he silently swore at the bird's daily announcement. He wanted more sleep, but he had to move quickly to the chicken coop. His first chore of the day was to secure his family's morning breakfast.

Later, he would be finished with this task and free to pursue and practice his dream. He was going to become a bull rider. He had seen many bull riding events at rodeos. He was acquainted with several bull riders, and one of his cousins was on the bull riding rodeo circuit.

His older brothers and father were calf ropers and steer wrestlers. Occasionally, they rode steers. But not bulls. They were smart to avoid this part of a rodeo. Bulls were flat-out dangerous.

It was the late 1940s. Electricity had not yet come to the family ranch, a remote enclave on the high plains of America's southwest. The house had only a wood-based fireplace in the living room and a coal burning oven in the kitchen. Thus, the boy reluctantly left the warm bed and placed his feet onto a cold wooden floor. The floor was constructed from unfinished planks of roughly hewn trees. Its smooth surface came from years of bare feet traipsing its surface and eventually polishing it to a dark brown sheen.

The rising sun had begun to bathe the room in a misty light. As night and day changed watches, the room he shared with two brothers began to show its form.

It was time to go to work. He dressed quickly, as much as anything to stay warm. His brothers remained somnolent. Their chores, more demanding than those of their younger brother, would come soon enough.

The boy was eager to secure the eggs, even if they were only one part of his family's meal. Leaving his bedroom, he bounded through the living room, the kitchen, then outside onto the house's porch. There, he picked up a pail that would hold the chickens' eggs. He headed for the chicken coop.

He got on well enough with his avian minions. The hens were passive creatures, and the rooster usually kept its distance if the child did not taunt it. If the rooster did attack, the boy would counter with a shout and a thrust toward the rooster. The bird would back away, continuing its haughty flaunting around the pen, but silently sulking because it had not cowed its adversary.

The first moments in the chicken coop pen—when the light was still modest—presented a different world. No warm beds or cold floors. Hay was scattered on parts of the ground, courtesy of the calves moving around and jostling with one another in the pen next to the coop. The coop itself had dirt floors, with more hay strewn about to absorb the offerings from the residents.

THE BULL RIDER

Dank from years of habitation, the chicken coop effused a deep, rich smell. Amazingly to the child, the hut was humid. The boy could not grasp how he could walk from the kitchen porch, some two hundred feet away, to the chicken coop, all the while experiencing the aridness of the high plains. Yet upon entering the coop, he would find himself in another world; a world of fecund and moist smells of aged hay, excrement, feathered creatures, and aging wood on the sides and roof of the pen.

The boy opened a small door to enter the chicken coop. Once there, the chickens gave him a desultory glance. They knew why he had come: to nestle them aside, to glide his hand underneath their bodies and steal their eggs. It was not unusual if the passive clucks from the chickens increased in frequency—if ever so slightly—when he placed his hands underneath the vulnerable parts of their bodies. To the boy, the sensuous warmth of the chickens' bottoms had the feeling of a soft glove.

On occasion, a hen was not acquiescent to his explorations. The boy suffered his share of pecks. But they were infrequent minor snips onto his hands and arms. The chickens had grown accustomed to the boy's forays. Their tolerance was helped along by his tossing grain into their nests after he had made his haul.

This chore was finished by his delivering a couple dozen eggs to the kitchen cook. She would fry the eggs for the boy's family and hired hands. Eggs, pork chops, biscuits, gravy, and fresh milk would fortify all hands for a morning of arduous labor.

The boy's next chore took place after breakfast. He was tasked with taking the plates from the large dining room table, and scraping left-over food into a slop bucket, one which also held the scraps from the previous day's lunch and supper.

The family kept a pigpen located near the chicken coop. Three pigs occupied the pen, so food scraps alone were not enough to fatten them up. Corn was added to the menu to round out the pigs' meals.

The morning was still young, not yet eight. The cool dry air was warming, and by noon, it would take on the character of an outdoor kiln. Unless the wind was up, and offering some relief, shirts and pants would soon be soaked in sweat.

The boy wished some of the summer heat would stick around to warm those chilly early mornings. But the high plains of America were not so indulgent to make life easy or comfortable for its inhabitants.

The previous evening, the boy's father had assigned chores for the workers' next day of labor. The boy was usually assigned less than glamorous tasks, such as painting fences and barns, hoeing a large garden, and cleaning horse stalls.

The hired men and older boys would spend the day tending to cattle, sheep, and horses. Yet their work was often less alluring than the bucolic scenes shown in movies. They spent many hours digging fence-post holes into the hard, rock strewn ground. They repaired windmills. They branded and castrated calves. They broke horses.

During these tedious hours, the boy filled his head with escapist thoughts by day dreaming about riding bulls. While hoeing the garden, he visualized being on the back of a bull. The animal was standing in the chute, edgily waiting for the gate to open. Once free, the bull would buck violently into the arena and dispense with its usually briefly mounted cowboy.

But this child was not to be a victim. Getting his grip on the braided bull rope, he nodded his head to direct the cowboys to open the gate and shout, "Let'em go, boys!" The bull would then explode from the chute, twisting and bucking. Sometimes with four legs off the ground, the bull contorted its body in what was called a belly roll. This maneuver often threw off the rider, leaving him on the ground and at the mercy of the bull's hoofs, horns, and massive body.

Without exception, the child's tiny frame stayed on the thousand-pound bull for the required eight seconds. He then dismounted and walked triumphantly toward the chutes to the cheers of the audience. While awaiting his next conquest to be loaded into the chute, he hoed another row of weeds.

Later in the day, after work was over, his brothers might help him ride the milk pen calves. Might, in that it was not a daily affair, as his brothers often spent their leisure time at the ranch's small arena practicing calf roping and steer wrestling.

The boy was a reluctant calf rider. He sought the big time: bulls...for which he had absolutely no experience. To complicate matters, the milk cow pen was small, with one side closed-in by a wooden shed. The calves were smart. They often ran alongside the shed, practically touching it. The boy was often scraped off the calf, resulting in wood splinters being lodged into his arm and leg.

After one of these scrape offs, he was dumped into a load of fresh cow dung. He could not visualize such a degrading outcome if he could ride his adversary, a bull. The huge animal would be a worthy competitor, not a mere calf, and the boy would ride his opponent in a real rodeo arena. Nonetheless, he kept plugging away. A few splinters and scraped skin were not going to deter him.

The boy was small for his age, but he was a wiry and strong lad. He could easily deal with paltry roosters, but he was not of sufficient physical stature to ward off another bird populating the ranch: the turkey. On occasion, a Tom would decide the child was walking too close to the turkey's turf. Or perhaps the Tom was just ornery. Whatever the reason, suddenly the turkey would come after the boy, who knew to get out of the bird's way. Unlike the gentle peck of the hen, or a phony attack from a small rooster, a big Tom's peck was painful.

He resented and came to hate the turkey. What humiliation! How could a bull rider be cowed by a bird? The boy was small, but his pride was not.

If possible, he avoided the turkeys, except on the Thanksgiving Day dinner. For more than one reason, he said "amen" after an adult had blessed a roasted turkey that was positioned in the middle of the dining room table.

The boy endured his brothers' teasing him about his splinter, manure filled calf rides. Yes, the child was prideful and also stubborn, but he was losing confidence in his riding abilities. If he could not ride a calf, how could he ride a steer, much less a bull? He was too young to know that success breeds confidence and what he needed was some success in his life. First, the crafty calves, then the pecking turkeys. What would come next?

The answer to his faltering ego was the local rodeo. Held several times a summer, his dad and older brothers were always contestants. And oh, those bull riders. They transported him back to his fantasies. He hoped he would someday be on exhibit in this huge and open showground.

His break came when his dad approached him during the bull riding event. The boy had been sitting on top of a fence overlooking the chutes and learning how the bull rider mounted the bull; how he adjusted himself onto the bull's back; how he fiddled with the rope until it felt secure and comfortable in his hand.

His father had watched his son's romps in the milk cow pen. On more than one occasion, he had pulled splinters out of the boy's body.

"Son, let's get some practice in a bigger pen. No fence sheds here."

THE BULL RIDER

The son was excited if unrealistically fanciful, "I can ride one of these bulls!"

"No, you're going to bust some muttons."

Another letdown. Mutton busting was a demotion from riding most anything on a ranch. A sheep did not buck. It ran hell bent for nowhere, usually randomly across the arena. Besides, the boy was nearing eight years of age. The children that contended in mutton busting were usually younger and often girls.

"Yes, sir." The boy had never refused a command from his father.

It is said that a person cannot become a success at meeting a quest if the person does not experience failure during this challenge. It is not only said, it is known to be true. But many people never come to understand this truism. If they experience only failure, how can they possibly know success?

The father knew the answer, leading to his directive to his son. He knew that to succeed in almost any endeavor, his son would have to experience failure, but success as well. From his rodeo experience, the father knew that during the time a new skill was being learned, failure-after-failure would crush the ego and stifle mental and physical efforts.

Yet success-after-success would not strengthen it either. Uninterrupted success would create a façade that could easily be stripped away when real challenges inevitably came along. Thus, the boy did as his father directed and entered the mutton busting contest to be held later that day.

Mutton busting was a straight forward event. At one end of the arena, a cowboy placed a child onto the back of a sheep. The sheep was shooed into the arena, usually running in a confused manner toward the middle of the grounds. The rider held on to the wooly back of the sheep for dear life, but more often fell-off after a few yards from the start.

The boy's experience with the larger and stronger milk pen calves prepared him well for mutton busting. He rode the mutton faultlessly. Eventually, the sheep gave up and stopped running.

The child dismounted his future bull and walked triumphantly across the arena to meet his family. Basking in the applause and shouts from the crowd, he had experienced success. Somewhere down the line, he knew he would upgrade to a more challenging competitor.

CHAPTER 31

BREAKING THE CHAIN

The family historian—a scholar in his own right—was now an old man. For decades, he had kept many pieces of documentation that chronicled the history of his family, going as far back as several years before the American Civil War.

He became interested in the seemingly erratic, even violent behavior of his relatives and their children during the years of the war and afterwards, especially during the Jim Crow days in which they were beaten, hanged, and nearly starved to death. They changed from a pre-war well adjusted family to a post-war family of dysfunction.

Yet during the recent generations, his family collectively altered their behavior—seemingly resembling their conduct during the pre-Civil War days. Some members of the family still carried chips on their shoulders. Some were incarcerated, but most of the males stayed out of jail and led nonviolent productive lives. Many flourished both intellectually and financially.

The word *seemingly* is used above, because he had to rely on his older ancestors' family correspondence. Those who could put pen to paper were prolific letter writers. After the war and during the Jim Crow era, their notes and letters sent to brothers, sisters, parents, and cousins often wrote about the dispiriting weariness of their thoughts and moods.

The man, a student of history, understood the well known and accepted theories of inheritance. He was aware that the changes he read about and observed in his family would have taken place through an evolutionary process that took centuries to come about, certainly not a few decades. But aspects of Darwinian inheritance had come under question.

Being a religious man, while he pondered his family's history and behavior, he reflected on Exodus 20:5: "Thou shalt not bow down thyself to them, nor serve them: for I the LORD thy God [am] a jealous God, visiting the iniquity of the fathers upon the children unto the third and fourth [generation] of them that hate me...."

He pulled out his Bible and reread, "...visiting the iniquity of the fathers upon their children." ...and for several generations.

To this man, iniquity implied injustice, even depravity. He continued to dwell on this seeming contradiction: *If my forefathers of some 17 decades ago performed deeds that led to their children being punished, how is it that my modern forefathers, even myself, are not laboring under the injustices of my ancestors? That they are not being punished? How is it that for our recent past, God seems to be less covetous of our bodies and souls? Something must be going on in our lives besides the punitive God from Exodus.*

The old man chanced upon a television program one day in which the commentator stated: "An increase in innate erratic behavior, even violent aggression, shows itself in the form of a human whose children's compositions lean toward being of the same nature as the parents. Recent studies reveal this behavior has a genetic basis. As examples, a father's aggression can be passed to the very next generation, as can depression, even alcoholism."[11]

The man thought: *Heretical! Darwin claimed such changes occurred through many years of mutations and natural selections. But one generation?*

Upon further study, he learned powerful environmental conditions (war, Jim Crow beatings, lack of food, even humiliation) left an imprint on the genetic makeup of humans. These genetic imprints could short circuit evolution and pass along new traits in a single generation.

The old man learned this science was known as *epigenetics*: heritable changes in how genes might express themselves because of factors other than the basic underlying DNA sequence. The process did not alter a genetic code, but the changes could be passed down to at least one generation and likely—if the conditions persisted—to subsequent generations.

As well, if conditions changed, so too might the person's epigenetic marks and the person's makeup.

These patterns of gene expression could come about because of a human's experiences with the environment. Specific chemical combinations called epigenetic marks sat atop genes and could instruct how the genes expressed themselves. Factors, such as recursive stress, smoking, over eating, and combat could create the genetic marks, which would then influence the children who had the marks passed to them by their parents.

---

[11] This part of the story is derived from Uyless Black, *2084 and Beyond*, Amazon.com, 2015. The quotes from the commentator are constructed by the author from accepted research.

The old man asked himself, *Then how did my recent relatives, even myself, turn ourselves around?* He learned that epigenetic markers were temporary, and they would disappear or change if environmental conditions changed.

However, during his reading about these subjects, he came across research that claimed people who migrated away from dysfunctional environments, such as ghettoes, were shown to have progeny who were less hostile, more social and successful than their forebears. That meant humans could change rapidly though the interactions between both nature and nurture.

Of course! This idea was common sense. It had long been known that children living in "better" neighborhoods fared better than their counterparts who came from ghettoes. Their parents had more wealth, which could promote them up the hierarchy of success. This situation wrought mental and physical benefits to their bodies and minds.

Slowly but surely, America's civil rights movement began to change the conditions and environments of African Americans. While a great number of African Americans languished in crime and misery, at the mercy of their debilitating backgrounds, many others were able to reorder their lives with new laws and the altered attitudes of many whites toward blacks.

By transitioning away from dangerous and underperforming walks of life, blacks and their children underwent mental and physical changes. The families who migrated from miserable conditions ended up having their epigenetics altered.

The man had finally come to understand the relatively rapid turnaround of his family and his family's fortunes. While paying silent homage to Frederick Douglass, Abraham Lincoln, Martin Luther King, and others he thought, *These men, and others like them helped break the chain of racial injustice.*

His thoughts turned to William Shakespeare, who in *The Merchant of Venice*, proclaimed, "The sins of the fathers are to be laid upon the children."

The old man ruminated: *Mr. Shakespeare was a bit of a plagiarist, but I suppose one need not provide a footnote to a Biblical source. But the Bible and Shakespeare had been only partially correct. The truth is, "The sins as well as the good deeds of their fathers are to be laid upon the children."*

CHAPTER 32

FASHIONING LIFE AND DEATH

On the first day after being deposited in a Hospice bed, the old man's remembrances of his vulnerability to aging came to mind. One such memory was when he was in his mid-thirties, playing wide receiver on a football team consisting of other former NFL wannabes. His teammates had played in high school, many in college. None of them came close to qualifying for an NFL team.

Such are dreams and their illusions. Nonetheless, during those days of long ago, a weekly game in a county recreational football league reinforced their love of the sport and maintained their desire to excel at it.

He was not exceptionally fast, but he was quick. Fast was speed over a wide expanse on the football field. Quick was speed within five to ten yards from the line of scrimmage. Quick required a powerful initial few steps. Fast required many of them, but perhaps not so powerful in the first couple strides.

It sometimes came down to the physical makeup of the runner. The longer range sprinters were usually of long, lean legs. The short range sprinters were often long in their body in comparison to their relatively short legs. But not always. Some of the world class, short yardage sprinters possessed compact and synchronized bodies—both in legs and torso.

Regardless of his bodily ratios, he was a favorite target for the quarterbacks' passes on short routes. He could easily out-thrust his defender from the line of scrimmage—at least for a few yards.

But there was more. He was one of the sure-handed receivers on the team. He had always possessed a gift, even from childhood, of somehow being able to catch a ball. For his football days, he boasted to various quarterbacks, "Just throw it near me. If I can touch it, I'll catch it."

Yes, a boast, but not an idle one. He had no recollection of ever missing an uncontested pass thrown to him during an actual contest.

Let's return to a county football league game of long ago. The quarterback called for a play in which the now Hospice patient was to sprint ten yards up the field, then execute a sharp turn toward the left side line, his favorite route. Off he went, straight forward for a few yards, then he cut to the left. His defender was backing up, expecting a long pattern. The ball was perfectly thrown, straight into his chest. He dropped it.

He could never recall missing such an easy pass in a game; occasionally in practice, but in a game, never! Nonetheless, the ball lay on the ground near his feet, ignominiously mocking his inexplicable failure.

His failure was a binary event, one that is expressed in one of two ways: yes or no; true or false; success or failure. On this occasion, his was failure.

Walking to the sideline, his teammates assuaged his dropped pass with words of encouragement. But the quarterback, a man who had played several years with him in recreational leagues, approached him on the sidelines, "What happened? Are you okay?"

This thirty-something year old man had experienced one of many win or lose experiences that had occurred in his life: catching, or in this situation, not catching a football in a contest. But the heart of the matter was that this one-time binary episode in his life had also been accompanied by many non-binary events in his existence—that is, many analog events.

Analog, because his life was also dictated by gradual changes to his being, of ongoing alterations to his body and mind. These aspects of his existence were continuously variable, and reasonably enough, undetectable to an indiscernible young man, or for that matter, any person. But their cumulative build ups led to this man dropping a football pass. He was growing old but was not aware of this process.

Binary: abrupt, discontinuous change. Analog: non-abrupt, continuous change. Yet early in his life, his existence revolved around high frequency, high amplitude, high energy experiences...analog experiences, imperceptible to a young body and mind.

Now, the old man, once a young sure-handed football player, lay in a Hospice bed. Sitting beside his bed was his son, Bill, now a middle-aged man. In his memory was his wife, who had occupied the same Hospice room two years ago.

His medicine laced dreams were pleasant: of his youth, his parents, his brothers and sisters, his friends, his football comrades, the dreams of his quarterbacks always knowing his hands could find themselves in the right vicinity of their throws. His other youthful exploits.

Yet, there were the binary events, events that gradually diminished his high definition analog life: Two broken backs from diving in college; a groin injury in the Navy; Agent Orange, courtesy of Uncle Sam in Vietnam.

His life was also replete with positive, successful events and experiences, whose cumulative binary actions accentuated his ongoing analog existence: a successful businessman; a respected citizen; a generous benefactor.

But now the man thought about the approaching time for his death. He knew his time on earth was clicking down on a final clock. It was an analog death watch, one that was gradual, and never endingly insistent. In perhaps an ironic twist, it was partially brought on by stand alone binary events.

First, in his seventies, there appeared the skeletal problems and pains that came from his youthful breaking of bones and assorted appendages during his many pursuits. During this time, he discovered these skeletal problems had damaged parts of his nerves, leading to pain and limited mobility.

Mother Nature had gradually brought forth other analog parts of life which had begun to assert themselves. In his late seventies, She took hold further, steadily blessing him with the cornucopia of old age: misbehaving kidneys, a malfunctioning prostate, clogged arteries—assorted presents from living beyond an overdue norm for growing older.

The father was awakening from his nap. Bill, "How's it going, Dad? Is there anything I can do for you?"

"Yes. Bill, do you recall our talks about the quirky nature of life; one filled with ongoing events, you know analog things… and others being binary, abrupt and sudden?"

"Sure, Dad. I have often thought about those conversations. I recall how so many, as you say, binary happenings affected your ongoing life—your analog life.

"You've fashioned your life, Dad! Your many stand alone accomplishments would put most of us to shame. Few people can do what you've done or even bother to try."

"Son, hand me the Alexander Dumas book. It's on the night stand."

"Which one, Dad. You've several of his books."

" 'The Count of Monte Cristo.' Turn to page 136. Read my underlines."

Bill reads, "…misfortune is needed to bring to light the treasures of the human intellect." "There's another underline, Dad."

"Please read it."

Bill reads further, "…from the collision of clouds, electricity is produced—from electricity, lightening, from lightening, illumination."

"I've had my share of clouds and illumination. But in this Hospice bed, I've far too many clouds on the horizon. It's time for my last binary experience, son. You say I've fashioned my life. Call the doctors in. Have them remove these tubes from my body. I'll fashion my death as well. We should all have the final say-so."

OTHER WORKS BY UYLESS BLACK

Lea County Museum Press:
The Light Side of Little Texas, 2011

 **Note**: Winner of 2012 Centennial award from The Historical Society of New Mexico for the "Best Book Depicting Domestic Life" in New Mexico.

Finalist for 2012 award from The New Mexico Book Co-op for "Non-fiction, other."

IEI Press:
A Swimmer's Odyssey: From the Plains to the Pacific, 2011
The Nearly Perfect Storm: An American Financial and Social Failure, 2012
2084 and Beyond, 2014
Digital Societies and the Internet: What the Present is bringing to the Future, 2016
The Cepee Dialogues: A Modern Fairy Tale, 2019
Read to Me With Ears to Hear and Eyes to See: Thirty-two brief stories, 2020

The following books (some of the first books on Internet protocols and architecture) offer historical perspectives on early data communications networks. Note the copyright dates.

SAMS:
Teach Yourself Networking in 24 Hours, 2009

IEEE Computer Society:
Physical Layer Interfaces and Protocols, 1988
X.25 and Packet Switching Networks, 1991

Prentice Hall/Pearson Publishing:

Data Communications, Networks, and Distributed Processing, 1983
Computer Networks: Protocols, Standards, and Interfaces, 1987
Data Networks: Concepts, Theory, and Practice, 1989
The OSI Model, 1991
Data Link Protocols, 1993
Asynchronous Transfer Mode (ATM) Networks, Volume I, 1995
Wireless and Mobile Networks, 1996
Emerging Communications Technologies, 1997
SONET and T1, 1997
ISDN and SS7, 1997
The Intelligent Network, 1998
Asynchronous Transfer Mode (ATM) Networks, Volume II, 1998
Asynchronous Transfer Mode (ATM) Networks, Volume III, 1998
Residential Broadband, 1998
Second Generation Mobile and Wireless Networks, 1999
Advanced Intelligent Technologies, 1999
The Point-to-Point Protocol (PPP), 2000
IP Routing Protocols, 2000
Internet Security Protocols, 2000
Quality of Service in Wide Area Networks, 2000
Internet Architecture, 2000
MPLS and Label Switching Networks, 2001
Internet Telephony, 2001
Voice over IP (VOIP), 2002
Networking 101, 2002
Optical Networks, 2002

McGraw-Hill:

TCP/IP and Related Protocols, 1992
Network Management Standards, 1992
The V-Series Recommendations, 1995
The X-Series Recommendations, 1995
Frame Relay Networks, 1998

Foreign Editions of Books:

Japanese: *Network Management Standards; Internet Security Protocols; Data Communications and Distributed Networks; IP Routing Protocols; TCP/IP; Multi-protocol Label Switching (MPLS)*
Korean: *Voice over IP (VOIP); Communications Networks: Protocols, Standards, and Interfaces*
Russian: *Communications Networks: Protocols, Standards, and Interfaces; Internet Security Protocols*
French: *Teach Yourself Networking in 24 Hours*
Chinese: *Advanced Features of the Internet; Voice over IP (VOIP)*
Spanish: *Data Communications and Distributed Networks; Communication Networks: Protocols, Standards, and Interfaces; TCP/IP; Advanced Features of the Internet*
United Kingdom: *Data Communications and Distributed Networks; Data Networks: Concepts, Theory, and Practice; Computer Networks: Protocols, Standards, and Interfaces.*

Magazine Articles:
Structured Programming:

InfoSystems magazine (circa 1975): "Gestalt Psychology Applied to Software Design" (An article explaining the brain's partitioning mental tasks to facilitate solving problems, based on Gestalt theory. A concept fundamental to a programming idea called structured programming, a revolutionary idea at that time.)

Metadata defined before it was named:

Data Communications magazine, November, 1980, McGraw Hill, Inc: "An Automatic Pilot for the Growing Distributed Network" (To my knowledge, the first known explanation of *metadata*.)

Subjects under research, with plans to publish:

Hot Wars, Cold Wars, and America's Warm War (working title)
My Capital, My America (working title)
The Light Side of Little Texas, Volume II

Short Stories:
Available upon request.

Essays available at Blog.UylessBlack.com:

America's Capital: Memories of author's experiences in Washington, DC.

America's Cities: Journeys and encounters in USA's towns and cities.

America's Finances: A series on issues such as Medicare, Social Security, and debt.

Computers and Networks: Essays on Internet "net neutrality" and software complexity.

Creatures and Computers: Drawing analogies to wildlife and Internet life.

Customs and Cultures: A look at America and Americana.

Eating and Drinking: Surveys of food fairs, cafes, and restaurants.

Food Effects and Drug Defects: Reports on toxic foods and drugs' side effects.

Foreign Affairs: America's relations with other countries.

Foreign Places: Taking roads, ships, and trains through parts of the world.

Immigration and Emigration: America's immigration practices and related problems.

Politics in America: With several reports on National Press Club speakers.

Presidential Places: Presidential homes, museums, and grave sites.

Privacy: NSA activities, right to Internet privacy in relation to other rights of privacy.

Sports and Games: Essays on competition and the beauty of sport.

Traveling America: Taking roads through America and America's cultures.

War Zones: Essays on cold, warm, and hot wars.

Listings of some newspaper articles. Uyless Black has published numerous articles on various topics with the local newspaper, *The Coeur d' Alene Press*. Here are some samplings:

- "When Political Correctness and Freedom of Speech collide," December 13, 2017.
- "The FCC Rulings on Net Neutrality," December 2-3, 2017.
- "What Walls Should America be Building?" November 1, 2017.
- "A Deeper Issue in Immigration Debate: Separation of Church and State," November 27, 2015.
- "Beware the Freedom to Kill the Freedom of Religion," November 28, 2015.
- "Muslims in America, a Personal Look," December 28, 2015.
- Ten articles about "The Internet and Society," January 4, 2016–January 15, 2016.

www.ingramcontent.com/pod-product-compliance
Lightning Source LLC
Chambersburg PA
CBHW070106280626
47159CB00016B/1488